Praise for 7

Winterbach is never afraid to take risks, to experiment with form
and style. Her work provides intellectual and aesthetic pleasure . . . There are
moments of sublime tenderness in her narratives which take your
breath away, and all you can do is sit in silent wonder, marvel as the
ordinariness and the mystery of our reality unfold right in front of
our eyes . . . [Her] writing has the astounding capacity to console, to find
meaning in a meaningless world. – Karina Szczurek, *Cape Times*

The quality of the writing, the quality of the characterisation, the oddity but
credibility of the world that Ingrid Winterbach creates in this
book – just turn the page, turn the page, turn the page, turn the page . . .
A hugely enjoyable local read. – John Maytham, *Cape Talk*

Praise for *It Might Get Loud*

What you get is a cacophony of realities. *It Might Get Loud* is a vast and
clamorous story that mixes the unmitigated presence of the dead, of demons
and spirits and mysteries, into the prosaic lives of the two main characters . . .
Intelligent, boundary shifting and unafraid of itself.
– Karin Schimke, *Business Day*

Fierce truth-telling . . . continuously exhilarating. – Patrick Lenahan

Praise for *The Road of Excess*

A fascinating and meditative read, and Winterbach's narrative is exquisite,
the prose as rich and textured as a 1980s velvet painting. – *Business Day*

A profoundly engaging and exhilarating read. – Jane Rosenthal, *Mail & Guardian*

Winterbach's writing is delight without respite.
– Michael Titlestad, *The Sunday Times*

Ingrid
Winterbach

THE TROUBLED TIMES
OF MAGRIETA PRINSLOO

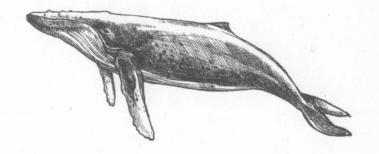

Translated by MICHIEL HEYNS

Human & Rousseau

Copyright © 2019 by Ingrid Gouws
English translation © 2019 NB Publishers
English translation by Michiel Heyns
First published in 2019 by Human & Rousseau,
an imprint of NB Publishers,
a division of Media24 Boeke (Pty) Ltd
40 Heerengracht, Cape Town, South Africa

First published in Afrikaans in 2018 as *Die troebel tyd* by Human & Rousseau

Cover design by Michiel Botha
Cover illustrations by Shutterstock
Typography by Nazli Jacobs
Set in 11.5pt on 16pt Caslon

Printed by CTP Printers, Cape Town

ISBN: 978-0-7981-7926-3
ISBN: 978-0-7981-7927-0 (epub)
ISBN: 978-0-7981-7928-7 (mobi)

For Chris Stander

One

Magrieta Prinsloo, daughter of the biology teacher, tall, firm of calf and buttock, dark hair, right eye inclined to wander slightly outwards when she's overworked, doctor of zoology, head of a laboratory with twelve people under her, in early January, after a run-up of several months, gradually grinds to a halt. A darkness, a deadly torpor, gradually takes possession of her. Japanese tantra, Tibetan art, start interesting her – the illustrations of the *terrible deities* fascinate her, with their fearful grimaces, their three eyes, their multiple arms, their left foot on the crushed skulls of the vanquished, the crowns and necklaces of skulls, the drums of human skin, the half-skulls brimming with blood. The darker the images, the better, the more closely she can identify with them. On the advice of a colleague she goes to see a psychiatrist. He prescribes a medication that does not have the desired effect on her state of mind. (Psychiatry is an art, not a science, he later exonerates himself.)

From one day to the next she is lifted out of her deadly torpor. She might as well have undergone electroconvulsive therapy, so huge is the change. At night she can see her hair standing up straight – a consequence of the electrical charge of her overactive synapses. For about sixteen weeks she's ablaze. She sheds furious tears – after seven dry-eyed months. She is like Chinnamasta, who chops off her own head to feed the parts of her divided self. She is like the goddess Kali, who has intercourse with the corpse of Shiva, a sword in one of her four hands, a lance in another, a half-skull in the last two. One of her feet is on the head of a tiger. Her hairless poes penetrated by the dead Shiva's stiff white cock.

No one dare confront her. An energy surges up from her cunt to her crown. It threatens to engulf her. Instead of apathetically depressed, as in the preceding months, she is now furiously depressed. Hectically, virulently depressed. She insults her department head (he is a myopic autocrat and a mediocre scientist, according to her); she publicly bad-mouths the department to which she's affiliated; she accuses the assistants under her in the laboratory of negligence, lethargy and general imbecility; she alienates her friends by her outspoken criticism of everything they say and do.

She slithers like an eel from the embrace of Willem, her husband. I would like to love you, she says, but I no longer can. My best intentions come to nothing. I long for the shelter of your arms, but as soon as you embrace me I feel suffocated, and I can't breathe. When she says it repeatedly, in a variety of ways, over a period of some weeks, he says, if that is how you feel, then we must start thinking about going our separate ways for the time being. Well then, she thinks, if it has to be it probably has to be.

The skull is her banner, the sovereignty of death her shield. She dreams of fire, of wriggling snakes, of raging storms, of people whose skins have been flayed.

She walks the streets on her own at night, during the day she walks on her own deep into the vineyard, she thinks, let *one*, let just *one* solitary soul *dare* to touch her. She'll decapitate them and chop up their bodies.

On every six-weekly visit to the psychiatrist he says, let's give the medication another six weeks to kick in properly. But when at last she's burnt all her boats and resigns from her job, she collapses into a dismal heap in front of him. I can't carry on like this! she shouts. I burn, I'm burning, I'm burning out. He clicks his tongue sympathetically, makes notes on his tablet, and prescribes a new medication.

This new medication calms her down and tempers her. But still she doesn't experience the feelings of fulfilment and deep inner peace that she'd hoped for. No relief. No conjunction of the male and female element in cosmic accord. Not in the least. She is chastised, pulled up short, sceptical, and unemployed – and that after a solid academic career.

She goes to stay for two weeks in a woman friend's holiday home at the sea. Then she gets up, responds to an advertisement in the paper, and applies for a position at the Bureau of Continuing Education.

*

In mid-May she washes her hair, applies lipstick and mascara, wears high-heeled shoes and a little pencil skirt, but she might as well have gone in slip-slops with unwashed hair, because during the interview Markus Potsdam, the director of the Cape branch of the Bureau, hardly looks up from his computer. The Bureau provides distance education to students. They have to be graduates to qualify for the course. It can be seen as a kind of bridging course between an undergraduate and a post-graduate education. This Cape branch of the Bureau has only recently been established and is not yet fully off the ground – start-up hitches still need to be addressed, says Potsdam. He's working on the snags. She has to recruit new associates, liaise with existing associates. That means she will have to travel, sometimes at short notice. In the Eastern and Western Cape, and sometimes to headquarters in Gauteng. Does she object to irregular hours? No. He sees she's well qualified. Can she concisely sum up her area of expertise? She worked on the evolutionary development of the phylum Annelida from the Ordovician era; on the earthworm, to be exact. The earthworm, he says, and glances up briefly. Yes, she says. Why the Ordovician? It is the peak period of the invertebrates. He nods curtly. Formally dressed in a long-sleeved shirt and tie. The shirt is slightly tight over the shoulders. Short dark beard, dark hair, dark eyebrows and eyes. (So different to Willem in appearance.) She would put him in his late forties, about her own age, perhaps a bit younger. He doesn't readily make eye contact and once, when their eyes meet, his gaze is painfully embarrassed. Why does she think she's suited to the position? She gets on well with people, she has many contacts in academic circles, she can process information quickly, she has a broad field of interests (she's not only an expert on worms; she's informed about art, she reads poetry). Why did she give up her – he glances at her CV in front of him again – successful academic career? She felt like a change (silent about the fiasco of the preceding four months). Fortunately he leaves it there. How good is her maths? Good enough, she says, but it depends – would she for instance have to be able to do a multivariable analysis? He glances up quickly again, gauges the comment, and takes note of the irony. Yes, for instance, he says. (She is thankful that he seems receptive to irony, at least.) Calculations, projections? he says. Not a problem, she says. When can she start? he asks. The next day, she says.

*

Magrieta's office is smaller than Potsdam's. They both have windows looking out on Stelloboschberg in the distance. The office of the secretary, Mrs Beetge, is next to Potsdam's. All three offices are accessible through a small reception area. Mrs Beetge has two red spots on her cheeks. Her hair is dyed a universal dark-red-brown shade and is straw-like in texture. Her eyebrows are accentuated by two slightly irregularly pencilled lines. She has a permanently startled expression; Magrieta is not sure whether the woman recognises her from one day to the next. But she's a fiend on the computer and her filing system is impeccable.

When Magrieta turns up in the morning, Potsdam is already in his office. Her first assignment is to liaise with Agent Dommisse, an associate responsible for their economics component. Agent? Did she hear correctly? Potsdam says it without batting an eyelid. Does he run this bureau like an espionage unit? For all she knows, she is now a secret agent. (A welcome change after her academic career.)

Magrieta and Willem are gradually reconciled. He is prepared to take her back after her manic-destructive period, when she told him that she had cut herself off from him in his embrace and could no longer find it in herself to love him. He is deeply wounded by her abrupt rejection of him in the preceding few weeks. He is shocked, he says, that she was prepared to throw an intimate relationship of fifteen years overboard, just like that. He doesn't know if he'll ever be able to trust her completely again. It doesn't convince him entirely that in her defence she blames the wrong antidepressant.

Willem is a straightforward, sober man, he does not wear his heart on his sleeve. His emotions run deep, as good as underground. He reacts fiercely to her rejection by shutting himself off from her. For a long time things are strained between them. With the greatest patience, tact and loving consideration she must overcome his resistance and regain his trust.

Two

In June Markus Potsdam sends Magrieta Prinsloo to the Eastern Cape to recruit a new associate there and to liaise with an existing associate (he refers to them respectively as Agents Oliver and Green). In addition there is another associate, a young woman from whom Magrieta must find out whether she's still coping, it seems she's struggling.

Magrieta doesn't relish the prospect of the trip, she's not sure that her new antidepressant is working. In PE a man and a woman are waiting for her when she arrives. The man holds up a tablet computer with her name on it. The woman is wearing a grey-blue coat of a cheap material. In the corner of the right side of her mouth she has an unsightly scar. It looks like a piece of torn material that's been sloppily sewn up so that the cloth pleats awkwardly in one spot. Magrieta sits in the back, the man and woman sit in front. In her right ear, she sees, the woman has a wad of cotton wool. An ear infection or a permanently damaged eardrum, she surmises.

In Albany West she is dropped at a guesthouse in the town. The owner, a worried young woman, offers tea and rusks. She warns Magrieta not to drink water from the tap, and that the water supply is sometimes cut off unexpectedly. It's cold. The wind blows. By half past five that evening it's so wet and blue outside that the world looks like an enormous aquarium. She receives a WhatsApp: *Everything is pandemonium. Nobody knows who's in bed with whom. Xander is apparently back from Pretoria, minus his memory and his sanity. But still serviceable as a figurehead.* She does not have the faintest idea who it's from.

It's a cold night full of wind and rain. Magrieta speed-reads a novel she finds on the bookshelf in her room. It is set in Tokyo. She opens *Endgame* by Samuel Beckett the way people open the Bible for an inspirational text. Her eye falls on the following words: 'I say to myself the earth is extinguished, though I never saw it lit.'

Despite a good night's rest she doesn't feel well the next morning. She meets Agent Oliver as arranged in a coffee shop in town. His name is Jerry Oliver, he is a palaeoclimatologist. He is there already when she arrives, reading something on his Kindle. He is in a wheelchair. Markus Potsdam did not mention this. She once read a novel in which the members of a terrorist group are all in wheelchairs. Very violent group. Political agenda. She takes a seat, shakes Agent Oliver's hand – cool and dry. Thinnish grey hair, moustache and neatly trimmed grey beard. Hooded eyes. He orders carrot cake and tea. She orders coffee. She has to recruit him as an associate. He will be responsible for a module on climate, among other things.

What is he reading? He's reading Heidegger. (All she knows about Heidegger is that he had Nazi sympathies.) A wheelchair terrorist with a philosophical bent, she thinks. She tries not to betray the fact that she's been wrong-footed. Not only by the fact that Agent Oliver is in a wheelchair, but also because she had expected him to launch immediately into an explanation of his area of expertise – how an inquiry into the climate of the Cambrian explosion could shed light on future climato-logical developments on earth. (She's well acquainted with the tricks of academics – stake their claim immediately and defend it to their dying breath.)

She has to keep the conversation going. Agent Oliver concentrates on his carrot cake and tea. Slightly hostile emanation, if she's not mis-taken. What's the carrot cake like? Not bad. Inside the room the light is dim. Outside the sky is grey. In her heart and head everything is also grey, she thinks. Perhaps the new pill. The grey descends from heaven and gradually infiltrates the coffee shop. It settles on everything: on Agent Oliver, on the other customers, on all the foodstuffs displayed on the shelves, on the periodicals, the day's newspapers, the walls, the posters of different kinds of cheese on the walls, on the floor, the ceiling.

The weight of the seeping greyness threatens to press her lungs flat. She assumes Markus Potsdam has been in touch with him, she says. He nods. And how does he feel about the possible association? she asks.

Agent Oliver dabs his mouth with a napkin, folds it, carefully puts it down and says: With all due respect, Miss, tell Markus Potsdam he can stuff his Bureau up his arse. For a few moments Magrieta is completely taken aback. So why then did you agree to meet me at all? she asks. To convey the message in person, he says. And now, if you will excuse me, and he picks up his Kindle.

Magrieta gets up, her legs a little shaky. She sits down again. What have you got against Markus Potsdam? she asks. Ask him when you see him next, says the man. You've wasted my time, she says. He shrugs. She gets up again, does not say goodbye, and quickly leaves the coffee shop. Outside, she looks right and left, and chooses a route. Down the street, right into a side street as far as the main street, past King Pie, Checkers, a bank, chemist, past street vendors selling watches, caps and all sorts of other goods, beggars, women with babies on their backs in front of the post office.

All the way to the poorer part of town she runs, passing to the right of the cathedral, ahead of the seeping greyness that's threatening to catch up with her. Her breath is racing. There is something violent brewing in the atmosphere. The wind starts blowing in spasmodic gusts. The sky is a treacherous greyish-pink, with sulphurous yellow undertones. This part of town is much busier than the upper part; she's on her way to a small Woolworths branch to buy a cleanser or something – anything. Cleanser, a coat, a jersey, anything. She hurries past shops like Edgars and Foschini (with a collection of synthetic red, royal-blue and mustard-yellow sweaters in the window), PEP and Jet. People, predominantly black, huddle together here and there on the pavement and impede her progress. A woman sits at something like an upturned disc plough on which she's cooking sausage and onions, the sausages like uncircumcised penises. At an entrance leading to a staircase a man holds a poster with photos of gold teeth and teeth with gold fillings. The man doesn't look South African – Nigerian? (All black suspects are always Nigerian.) A morose teenager with enormous thighs brushes past Magrieta. A man wants to sell her a cellphone.

When she hears screams behind her, she turns around, just in time to leap, with the others, out of the way of a man in a wheelchair charging furiously at them. Magrieta and a woman in a cap with faux-fur earflaps almost end up in each other's arms. As far as the man moves along the pavement, people jump out of the way, shouting at the man and swearing at him in Xhosa. He takes no notice and disappears around the corner. For a moment Magrieta had thought it was Agent Oliver pursuing her with grim intent, but realises that it was a much younger man, his cheeks pink with cold.

She returns to the guesthouse and sleeps. She has an appointment at half past three with Agent Green. She waits for him at a coffee shop – a different one from the one where she met Agent Oliver that morning. After an hour he has still not turned up, and she can't reach him on his cellphone. The wind blows even harder. Magrieta almost literally blows through the town – coat and scarf flapping in the wind. At five o'clock she is blown into the guesthouse. The force of the wind intensifies. It starts raining hard. Soon the wind is blowing so fiercely that it looks as if the trees are being bent horizontally. It rains unremittingly. She waits for Agent Green to contact her. At half past six the owner knocks gently at Magrieta's door. They have prepared Thai food, would she perhaps like to join them? She is grateful for the invitation.

After supper she reads a few poems in a small William Blake collection she finds on the bookshelf in her room. She reads among others the poem about the sick rose. She and her ex-husband used to listen to Benjamin Britten's setting of it. She thinks it's an appropriate poem for the stormy night out there. After all, she has a special relationship with the worm, whether it penetrates the heart of the rose metaphorically or not. The worm remains her thing, even though she's tried to renounce it.

The wind blows an incessant gale. In the night it blows so fiercely that she fears the roof will be blown off. She sleeps restlessly. At times she thinks, now, *now*, the roof is blowing away, in this howling storm, with the invisible worm flying somewhere, searching for the rose's bed of crimson joy.

*

The next morning everything is still. The storm has abated. Agent Green is still not answering his phone. She SMSes Markus Potsdam: *Green has disappeared off the face of the earth and Agent Oliver is reading Heidegger.*

Potsdam responds: *Don't be put off by agents' monkey tricks or dubious reading tastes.*

Her last appointment is with Agent Jansen van Rensburg, in the same coffee shop where she met Agent Oliver. The space is less gritty than she left it yesterday, but the mood becomes more desolate by the half-minute. Through the window she sees mainly beggars, car guards and young people who look like students walking by. On the narrow stoep is a white bougainvillea in a pot. Across the street, directly in her line of vision, is a whitewashed building with an enclosed façade. Magrieta has been in town since early morning; she knows she must keep moving. Agent Van Rensburg has let it be known that she will be wearing a red scarf.

At ten past three a blonde woman in a red scarf appears. Hair page-boy style. Very thin. Knock-knees. She makes a beeline for Magrieta. She introduces herself as Nonki Jansen van Rensburg. Would she like to drink something? Yes, please. She rubs her hands, reddened, in finger-less gloves. She has a book with her – *Bizarro Fiction: An Introduction.* There's a lecture on it this evening in the English department, should Magrieta be interested. Yes, why not? Okay, Nonki will come to pick her up. Their tea arrives. Nonki eats hungrily. She talks a lot. She's responsible for a literacy and drama project in the township, under the auspices of the Bureau. She grew up in Modimolle. (The place where the monster committed his atrocities, Magrieta remembers.) Her parents were anti-apartheid activists. They managed the local cell of the SACP. They *were* the local cell. When they had to flee across the border to Botswana, she went to boarding school in the town. It was still Warmbad then. The pits, she says. It was the most terrible time of her life. (She looks younger than she probably is. She holds her cup in both hands. Still wearing the half-gloves. Her fingers are red as if the blood circulation isn't good. A common condition in people who are too thin.) The other children – Afrikaans children – treated her as if she were a leper. They said her parents were kafferboeties and she had a kaffer name. After a year she moved to a convent school in Mbombela, the old Nelspruit, when her parents went to Mozambique. Two things she no longer does, she says. The one is speaking Afrikaans, and the other is appealing to the Virgin Mary – been there, done that, got the T-shirt. (Small titties, Magrieta surmises.) Her mother later lost a leg in a bomb explosion in Mozambique, but now both her parents are dead.

And how is the project in the township going? Nonki shrugs, it's not easy, she says. Conditions are challenging. People are struggling. There's a lack of basic provisions. It's a damaged community. It gets her down some days, but she's still keeping up, only just.

That evening Nonki comes to pick Magrieta up at the guesthouse. The speaker is a guest in the English department. She's from Iceland (blew in with the eruption of the volcano Eyjafjallajökull). She looks like Björk. The lecture room is cold. The students stand around shivering and rubbing their hands. On the walls are large photographs of English-speaking South African writers: among others, Alan Paton, J.M. Coetzee, Nadine Gordimer and Bessie Head. The Björk double talks about Bizarro fiction. Her English is well-nigh unintelligible because of the multitude of s-sounds, rolled r's, and the l-sound that sounds like the tl-sound. After her talk everybody repairs to a party at a student house. Magrieta lets herself be borne along like a leaf on water. Gusts of rain, icy wind.

Up a hill to the digs. In the sitting room a whole lot of people are already huddled together. There are two couches covered in Lesotho blankets, for the rest plastic chairs. A typical student house with a motley assortment of posters on the walls. In the kitchen the dishes are piled up in the sink. Hygiene doesn't look great. It's a night of storms in the Eastern Cape with the worm that flies in the howling wind.

Magrieta knocks back a few glasses of wine in quick succession, because she's cold. She has no appetite for the peanuts and dry biscuits. In the press of people Magrieta comes face to face with the Icelandic author. She now sees clearly that the woman is none other than Björk. She looks so much like Björk that it might as well be the woman herself. Magrieta asks her if she also sings and the woman says, yes. She asks if she sometimes wears plastic dresses and the woman says, yes. She asks if the volcano is still active and the woman says, yes. Do they speak only one language in Iceland and the woman says, yes. What does she write? Magrieta asks. She rewrites the Old Norse and Icelandic sagas with a Bizarro twist, says the woman. (It's possible that she says or means something else.) Icelandic's near-isomorphism to Old Norse means that Icelanders can read the Eddas, sagas and other Old Norse literary works from the tenth to the thirteenth century without difficulty (she is once again not quite sure whether that is exactly what the Björk woman is saying). How fascinating, says Magrieta, rocking forward and back on her feet, and gazes mesmerised into the woman's near-black eyes, almost without eyelids, with the prominent epicanthic fold, also known as the Mongolian fold, so different from the eyes Magrieta is used to. Do they eat moss in Iceland? she asks.

Somebody seizes her by the arm. The room is dense with smoke. The person introduces himself as Basil Green. Agent Green, therefore. Where *were* you? she asks, we had an appointment. Small mouth, gibbous cheeks, his lips clenched shut, determined, as if he's guarding a secret. I was ill, he says, I'm sorry I didn't get in touch with you. He seems unwell indeed. His face is pale and his skin is unhealthily blotched. We must talk, she says. He nods. His mouth opens and shuts, it looks as if he wants to say something, but has second thoughts.

She excuses herself, she has to get to the toilet urgently. For that she has to walk through the kitchen. Not only does the bathroom lead straight out of the kitchen (in defiance of building regulations), but there are quite a few electrical cords hanging about, apart from the naked flex to which the bulb is attached – lethal. On the wall above the bath is written:

If man does not take pleasure in killing, he becomes an animal

Beneath it somebody else has written:

What about women you cunt

In the kitchen a woman is busy at the stove. She's wearing a long black skirt and a black jersey, and she has long black hair. The gas flame on which she is cooking something in the pan (something vegetarian?) is almost a metre high. Magrieta shudders. This house is a deathtrap. The woman is holding a book she's reading while frying the single patty. Magrieta asks her what she's reading. Wordlessly the woman shows her the book's title page: *Thus Spake Zarathustra.* How are you finding it? Magrieta asks. Nietzsche is *everything*, the woman says, without looking at Magrieta. Okay, Magrieta says. (She quickly sends Potsdam an SMS: *People take their philosophers seriously in this town.* He retorts: *Another reason not to trust them.*) She looks for a clean glass to have a drink of water, her mouth is dry and her head is humming. Here in the kitchen merriment reigns.

When Magrieta gets back to the sitting room, she sees, out of the corner of her eye, on the other side of the room, a man in a wheelchair. Not Agent Oliver and also, as far as she can determine, not the man who tilted yesterday at full speed through the people on the pavement. She moves on, through the throng of people, past two more men in wheelchairs, when suddenly somebody else blocks her passage. A man, so dark of skin that she can hardly distinguish his features in the poor light. He just wants to congratulate her on her work, he says. Even the whites of his eyes are dark. His mouth is big, mobile and expressive. For an instant Magrieta has no inkling what he's talking about. In Venda we regard you very highly, he says. My students have the greatest admiration for your research. You must come and visit us, he says. I'll send you an invitation. Her worm research, she realises. Her previous life. Gladly, she says. She does not say that she's ceased her research and left the department in disgrace. (Somebody else is now continuing her respected research; is now investigating the evolution of the earthworm's rudimentary nervous system.)

He introduces himself, Professor Mogoerane, head of the zoology department at the University of Venda in Thohoyandou. She knows of him, he is a palaeozoologist. She shakes his hand. As she starts making out more of his features in the dim light, she sees that he looks like a nice guy. Quite a wry flicker in the eye. And the lovely, large, generous mouth, of which the inner lip is quite a bit pinker than the very dark lip edge. She stares spellbound at it. A determined mouth, but also the mouth of a hedonist.

And what is he working on? she asks. He and his students are engaged in a large new project, they are very excited about it. It's actually not common knowledge yet, but they have a site near Makhado, in the Soutpansberg. He can almost say with certainty that it dates from the Middle Cambrian. Perhaps as rich as the Burgess Shale. A first for South Africa. They are very proud and excited, he says again.

He glances over his shoulder, then leans closer to her, his generous mouth by her ear: They are careful about letting it be known just yet, but one of their earliest finds is a fossil that looks very much like the *Opabinia*! Five eyes, he whispers in her ear, can she believe it, and the same proboscis snout! Can that be?! she exclaims in surprise. He smiles triumphantly. She must come and have a look, he says. They would very much like to have her on site. They have the highest opinion of her expertise. His inner lip such a surprising bright pink, and the mouth so extraordinarily firm and well defined. Wonderful, she says, she'd like to come – she's never been in the Soutpansberg. He gives her his card. She slips it into her handbag, says goodbye to him, and tries to catch Nonki's eye.

It's time to go home. She is tired. But Nonki is rapt in conversation with a sinewy fellow with dreadlocks on the other side of the room. The man makes strange snake-like movements with his body, it looks like he's having trouble staying upright, in fact, while Nonki is talking to him passionately. From his glazed expression it's clear that he's high, stoned to the eyeballs. Magrieta grabs Nonki's arm, it's late, please can they go home, but Nonki is not to be torn away from the spaced-out fellow. He is recklessly handsome, with the sleazy good looks of a pimp or a small-time drug pusher. Lanky body, unfocused eyes. He directs his glazed gaze at Magrieta and says, 'What is this, my sister, come join us.'

Agent Green offers her a lift back to the guesthouse. It's icy outside, but at least it's not raining any more. Who is the guy that Nonki is so taken with? she asks. It's Robert Raditsela, a poet, high profile here and abroad. He writes poems in Setswana and English.

She has to shut one eye to focus, her head extravagantly light from all the wine on an empty stomach.

He is a poet himself, Agent Green confesses bashfully. Oh lovely, says Magrieta. She has to work hard not to vomit, it must be from the cold and the booze. Agent Green gesticulates with his hands while he speaks. The palms of his hands and the first digit of his fingers are fleshy, the fingers are spaced out wide on the palm and bend far backwards. His hands remind Magrieta of the illustrated hands she saw in a book on Japanese tantras, when she was in the enraged phase of the first anti-depressant.

What is it with all the people in wheelchairs in this town? she asks. Oh, he says, there's a convention of wheelchair users at the university at the moment. Is Agent – is Dr Oliver part of it? she asks. No, he says. A convention of wheelchair users. Well then. The group in the novel used extremely violent methods. A terrorist group with a radical political agenda. Agent Green gesticulates with his tantric hands, but she doesn't hear a word he's saying. She's too cold, too nauseous, too drunk, too far gone down some false trail or impassable road. What is she doing in the middle of the night, in the Eastern Cape, on some half-baked mission? For some time now, she's been out of her element, out of her depth.

'Stop the car,' says Magrieta. 'I need to throw up.'

She gets out just in time and stands next to the car. She bends over. She presses her hands to her knees. Her ribcage contracts violently. She throws up a clear stream of sour liquid. Above her beleaguered and impeded head Spica, Arcturus, Vega and Altair are prominent in the night sky.

When she's done, she wipes her mouth with the back of her hand. Her teeth chatter. She leans one hand against the roof of the car. She's made a mistake. She belongs in the Soutpansberg, she belongs on her knees with Professor Mogoerane and his team in search of fossils from the Middle Cambrian. She belongs in her own laboratory, in a white coat, behind a microscope. She should be immersing herself in the evolution of the nervous system of the phylum Annelida from the Ordovician. Her loyalty lies with the earthworm. *That* is her calling, that is where she belongs. In the Ordovician, not in the middle of the night in the Eastern Cape on a ridiculous mission and a useless antidepressant. She should keep her attention focused, unfaltering, on the unfathomability of the Hadean aeon, on the billions of years it took the first multicellular organism to develop. What possessed her to give it all up? Should she sue the psychiatrist? Should she send Markus Potsdam an SMS right now that she's resigning?

She gets back into the car. Her teeth are still chattering. Are you okay? Agent Green asks solicitously. 'Yes,' she says. 'You can go.'

*

At five o'clock the next morning Magrieta gets up. She feels nauseous and woozy. At six o'clock she's picked up by the same man who brought her here. It's still dark, and it's cold. His girlfriend is with him again. She's wearing the same coat. Magrieta sees that it's not blue-grey, but a very pale blue, paler than powder blue. In the dark she can't see the woman's scarred mouth very well. She can also not see whether she has a cotton-wool wad in her ear again. The young man is wearing only a short-sleeved shirt, despite the cold. The road is busy for this time of morning. They must be driving in a southwesterly direction, because diagonally behind them the sky is slowly changing colour. Magrieta half-reclines with throbbing head and numb neck in the back of the car. From time to time she surfaces from her befuddled semi-sleep and looks through the window at the landscape speeding past. Extensive grassland with copses of trees in between. She asks the man what he's going to do for the rest of the day. He's going back to fetch one more person in the town to drop at the airport. Then he's going to take Cornelia (the scarred woman) for breakfast at the sea. Then he's going to buy nuts for his squirrels. Two squirrels that he keeps in a cage. What are their names? Magrieta asks. Poppy and Poopy, he says. She hopes Poopy doesn't live up to his name, she says, but the man does not hear her.

In Cape Town she takes the shuttle. It drops her at home. Willem is still in bed. She throws off her scarf, takes off her jacket, her jersey, her skirt, she takes off her boots. She gets into the warm bed with him, in her shirt, leggings and socks. He enfolds the two of them in the duvet. The warmth is beneficent. Her cold hands warm up quickly. He lies behind her. Her buttocks fit into his pelvis. He slips his hand under her vest. A dreaminess overtakes her, she reverts to a primitive state. Fused in the warm bed they become one organism with a gradually slowing metabolism. She can't even think about having to get up. A cruel casting back into the world, anew.

'Forgive me,' she murmurs. He makes a small bodily movement that she interprets as, it's fine, we leave what's happened behind.

The next morning, first thing, she goes to greet Markus Potsdam. As always when she comes into his office, he lurches to his feet. Did you give them hell? he asks. For sure, she says. That's good, he says. Agent Oliver has a message for you. Yes? He says you can stuff your Bureau up your arse, she says. Oliver is a cripple with a chip on his shoulder, says Potsdam, unruffled. Is that a politically correct pronouncement? she asks. He meets her gaze, smiles just barely and says: Personally I find political correctness a pain in the posterior.

She feels light-hearted when she leaves his office, pleased that she and Potsdam have covered a bit of ground.

Three

Back in town at the end of June, Magrieta takes a late-afternoon walk in the vineyard above their house. She usually walks with Willem, but when he's working late she walks on her own with the dog. She's not supposed to venture too deep into the vineyard on her own (the peril of undesirable elements), but with the dog she feels safe. She prefers walking alone sometimes, because when she's walking with Willem she's less alert to her surroundings.

She walks along the neat pathways between the vines, and then along one of the dirt tracks past the back of the school building. The whole area here is strewn with rubbish. She doesn't know who's responsible for this. The pupils certainly throw their chip packets and sweet papers here, and empty cool-drink cans, but where do the lengths of cracked plastic piping, chips and chunks of concrete (something or other demolished to the last brick), smashed liquor bottles, empty plastic bottles, discarded garments, hair curlers come from? Who is living here, who wanders through this area, who leaves their piles of excrement, pools of vomit, traces of blood, bodily fluids, plastic containers and bags, gnawn-bare chicken bones, old shoes, torn underwear here? She comes across a heap of used sanitary towels, and a large heap of ash – everything transmogrified unrecognisably by the flames. Only just identifiable are a blackened orange and a charred carrot. Everywhere on these late-afternoon hikes she sees signs of human habitation – remains of fires, burrows dug out in the ground under shrubs, but she never sees inhabitants.

It is winter, getting colder. How do these wanderers protect themselves against the cold, against the squalls of rain that sometimes carry on for days? Never does she see anything resembling a tent shelter, or a burrow in the ground covered with plastic.

Here an underground life is lived, under the radar of standard middle-class privilege. Only traces are left – the single shoe, the garment half-covered in soil. Once something nylon-ish, in blue and purple with pink diagonal stripes. She kicks against it with her shoe, tries to pick it up with the tips of index finger and thumb, is repelled by it, a woman's blouse of synthetic material, half-covered in caked mud.

What is the language, the coded utterances of these people? She imagines she can sometimes hear the echo of it on the wings of the wind – the secret argot of the poes. Poes, go. Poes, come. Poes, fuck off.

In the sky, an enormous cunt, like the eye of God.

Four

Characters who get into cars and drive to places where things happen to them – pleasant as well as unpleasant things. Like being shadowed by a stalker, or attacked and robbed in the street, or falling and being injured. Or receiving a phone call that changes their life. Or starting to hallucinate behind the wheel of their car and being unable to drive on. Or going to meet the object of their desire (sexual desire), hopeful, but also with a paralysing feeling of foreboding, and this person finally rejects their advances. ('I'm sorry, you're a good friend, but more than friends we cannot be.') Or a character at the end of her tether, on the spur of the moment or even with premeditation, against the dictates of her own reason, commits a deed that alienates the love object even further from her and leaves her emotionally wrecked or even irrevocably displaced. Or a character can amble next to the sea, on the horizon a sinking ship of which he is not even aware. Such a character could walk next to the sea and come across the washed-up carcass of a seal or even a whale. He then gazes in disbelief at the gigantic animal and – confronted with the dead leviathan from the ocean's depths – understands something about himself as an earth-bound, two-legged mammal, as well as his place in the scheme of things. The animal inevitably reminds him of the Biblical leviathan, and Jonah who is swallowed by the fish and spat out again after three days. Jonah who sojourned for three days in the belly of the largest mammal on earth – no half measures for God: If you won't hear, you must *feel*. There was a command to obey, and obey it you will.

A character can travel to a destination with the intention of taking his own life there. He can park the car on a deserted dune, stumble down the dune, walk across the narrow strip of sand, and wade into the ocean.

Perhaps his eye can fall at the last moment on a lovely shell, which momentarily stops him in his tracks, his intention temporarily snagged. But already half-dazed from the pills he took, or the alcohol he drank, to soften his dreadful resolve, he can leave the shell behind and stumble on. Or he can walk into the sea terrifyingly sober, spurred on by his will alone. Or he can drive to a cottage at the sea, kindly made available to him by a friend, and take his own life there – by shooting or hanging himself, or taking an overdose of pills. The cottage just remote enough so that he is found only after several days, and sometimes by pure chance, and then on account of the warm weather is barely identifiable.

Or a character can decide that the only way of gaining control over her life would be to go and stay for a while in isolation in a friend's beach cottage. Periods of isolation are often recommended for people under emotional strain – away from the allure of Facebook, newspapers, Twitter and the like, as well as the manifold and stressful demands of loved ones, children, spouses, beggars and friends. But not everybody can survive emotionally in conditions of extreme isolation. Whether in a wooden hut in a forest, a mountain chalet, or a cottage at the sea, such a person can, on arrival, or within the first hour or two, realise it was a mistake. She had hopelessly romanticised the idea of a lone retreat to bring her to her senses. Panic-stricken, she realises that she can't sustain it. The isolation throws her back upon herself with the force of a thing being flung against a wall – an object, like a glass, or a plate, or even a pet animal. He is overtaken by melancholia, by an experience of the abyss in himself, a place so bleakly desolate that no healing influence can emanate from it. This sensation of desolation can be so menacing that the person succumbs to a state of panic, becomes paralysed, and withdraws into sleep. Or decides to leave everything right there and walk into the ocean, or to hang himself from the railing in the shower.

Five

Magrieta finds Markus Potsdam interesting. He is reserved. Severe, even, and a bit blunt at times, but with a certain awkwardness tempering his severity. He may even be shy. He doesn't readily make small talk. All the more surprising, then, his laid-back, ironic SMSs, and his sometimes unexpected, subversive asides. Because she doesn't know anything about him, she cautiously sounds out Mrs Beetge. But the woman is not to be drawn. It's always been her policy, she says, not to delve into the personal lives of her employers. And she and Mr Potsdam haven't been working together for all that long in any case. Can she at least say whether he's married? Magrieta asks. No, says Mrs Beetge, not as far as she knows.

Although after the winter solstice the July days are already growing longer, it doesn't feel like it yet. It still gets dark early, and Magrieta and Willem often walk the dog in the rich twilight: the vines, newly pruned, are bare, the mountains sometimes wreathed in drifts of mist. When they go walking in late July after sunset on a cloudy day, the mountains are dark, massive, the dominant colours are dark blues and greens, not a trace left of yellow and red tints, although the bare vines have a grey-purple sheen.

In August she is instructed by Markus Potsdam to get in touch with Professor Deneys Swiegers. He is attached to the Department of Engineering, an expert in the field of artificial intelligence and neural networks. He is constructing a duck – a soft robot, he explains, its control system based on the principles of neural networks, which share certain characteristics with the functioning of the brain. Magrieta likes to think of it as a mechanical duck (which of course it is not). Why not rather construct a soft robot woman, she wonders, that would surely be much more interesting than a duck. Deneys Swiegers has an open face, a high forehead and clear eyes.

In August too, also as instructed by Potsdam, she has to have lunch with two of their most important donors. Make sure you look sexy, he says, these guys make big donations. (By now she's used to his deadpan pronouncements.)

'Blow jobs for both as dessert?' she asks.

'You needn't go that far,' he says.

The one donor has a big head and a thick neck, but his features are set much too close to one another in his large, fleshy face. Something reptilian. The other donor is one of those Afrikaner men Magrieta associates with the uncles of her childhood: brusque, patriarchal, moustached, with a belly, a suntanned neck, thick, hairy fingers – the uncles she associates with her burgeoning sexual awareness – confusion, revulsion, fascination, sexual titillation. She remembers one such incident. On the farm of one of her aunts. The aunts, adult women, covertly muttered to one another: Creepy, a pervert. She'd not understood how, perhaps it wasn't even spelt out, but something deviant was hinted at; her interest was piqued. At night she fantasised. The full moon lit up the yard. There was an intensity of unarticulated sexual yearning (which may never have been equalled in her adult life). The one donor's massive fortune was built on cellphone masts erected in the rest of Africa, and the other's on exporting tinned food and cigarettes to African countries (a Lucky Strike empire). They talk business. When they focus on her, they are exaggeratedly gallant. (The hand sometimes on her leg.) They pour her too much wine, order more courses when she's long since had enough, make unsubtle sexual innuendos, then become absorbed in their own business talk again. She is charming and coquettish. (Now I'm a glorified PRO and whore, she thinks, why doesn't Potsdam eat with these important donors himself?)

When she escapes to the toilet, she finds, written in black koki pen behind the door: BE MINDFUL OF THE LEVIATHAN. With a strange little schematic representation underneath – a kind of pictogram – that she can't decipher; something between a Zeppelin, an amoeba and a whale. She takes a photo of it with her cellphone.

In September Magrieta has strong reservations about her job at the Bureau. She doesn't think she can keep it up much longer. She likes Potsdam, although they have little personal interaction (they haven't even had coffee together in the coffee shop one floor down), but the work doesn't really interest her. She misses her research, she misses the laboratory. She watches the newspapers closely for jobs in her field, but for the time being there are no vacant posts in the province. As long as the man she insulted so profoundly remains head of zoology, she can forget about ever being re-employed there. In the vineyards the first signs of life are burgeoning: the sap starts rising in the bare vines and here and there delicate shoots are showing.

When at the end of October she's once again having coffee in town at the Fynbos Coffee Shop, she finds written behind the door in one toilet, again in black koki pen: BEAR IN MIND THE LEVIATHAN. Again with the strange little pictogram – the Zeppelin, amoeba and whale.

In November Potsdam sends her to Gauteng to attend a conference on distance education. For weeks the region has been in the grip of a debilitating heat wave. The papers are boring. Her attention strays. She dreams she falls down a mine shaft and ends up in the Hadean period where there is nothing. (Why does paradise bloom but hell is infertile?)

In mid-November Magrieta reads in the newspaper that Professor Eliot Mogoerane, head of the Department of Zoology at the University of Venda, has been shot in a hijacking and airlifted to a hospital in Pretoria, where he's fighting for his life. She is upset. She had still cherished the hope of going fossil-hunting with him and his team sooner rather than later: the southern equivalent of *Anomalocaris* – with the winged mouth and teeth on the inner edge, and *Odontogriphus* – the toothed riddle, with traces of small cone-shaped teeth, among others.

In the days that follow she can find no news reports indicating whether Professor Mogoerane survived the hijacking. She assumes he did, otherwise his death would surely have been reported.

When at the end of November she's having a meal at a posh wine estate on the outskirts of the town, with a lovely view onto olive orchards and sky-high mountains, behind one toilet door (disfiguring the impeccably clean, state-of-the-art bathroom) there is written, once again in black koki: CONSIDER THE LEVIATHAN. And once again with the little pictogram.

The young green bunches of grapes have started appearing already.

In December she is given a big bonus and three weeks' leave.

Six

Early in January Mrs Beetge needs a hysterectomy unexpectedly. A new secretary has to be appointed in her place. Instead of a secretary Magrieta acquires an assistant who, according to Markus Potsdam, will make chicken feed of the secretarial work. Isabel Durandt is tall, almost as tall as Magrieta. Pretty. Clear eyes, pale skin, level-headed, ironic. (A year or two younger than her own daughter.) Not someone to be thrown off balance easily, as Magrieta reads her – a cool customer. Abundant wealth of hair, the colour of honey. Long limbs, fingers elegantly tapered, the fingertips pointed like those of imperial Japanese courtesans. She has recently completed a master's degree in computer science, concentrating on neural networks, and is waiting to continue her postgraduate studies at MIT. Magrieta is initially sceptical – how can Potsdam expect such a highly qualified person to do basic secretarial work, but the girl says she's grateful to find something temporary before continuing her studies overseas. She is indeed a wizard on the computer. She's so quick that her long courtesan fingers hardly touch the keyboard, and there's no computer problem she can't solve instantly. She helps Magrieta with scheduling, and with more everyday tasks like writing emails, arranging flights, making bookings (because Magrieta's duties are ever increasing). Magrieta is pleased to have got an assistant with such a command of the expertise and technology of the future.

In mid-January Potsdam sends Magrieta to the West Coast on a mission to Jameson Bay, just north of Vredenburg. He says that for the time being it's not important who the person is she must meet there – he'll contact her as soon as she gets there. (Person – did Potsdam say person, not agent?!)

'It all sounds very mysterious,' she says. 'I trust that in due course all will be revealed to me. Is this still a Bureau matter or are you expecting an illegal delivery?'

'There's nothing illegal about it,' says Potsdam curtly. (He seems to be in a particularly bad mood this morning. She has no idea what it could be connected with.) Just make sure she's there, he says. The person will get in touch with her. He would do it himself, but he has other obligations. (Other obligations – you don't say.)

'I shouldn't perhaps take a weapon along?' she asks, to provoke him.

'If it will make you feel better,' he says.

'You run this bureau like an espionage unit,' she says.

'If you say so,' he says, but he's not to be drawn this morning – doesn't even look up from his computer. As soon as she thinks she's won some ground with him, she loses it again – one step forward, two steps back. One day he is approachable, the next incommunicative. It frustrates her.

'Take your assistant along if you feel like it,' he says. 'Think of it as a breather.'

Magrieta decides they might as well make an outing of it, as Potsdam suggested, and she invites her friend Jakob Wolmarans along as well. She knows he's battling with the novel he's writing. He wrote a beautiful first novel about a man dying of fever on the banks of the Olifants River. Towards the end he's eaten by a crocodile. Very violent, almost surreal. Very well received. Jakob is sturdily built, superfit, a black belt in karate, was a good sprinter at school, but he's never been able to handle the pressure of competition, he says. Shoulder-length light-brown hair; sometimes wears a bandana. Soft eyebrows, prominent, pouting lower lip. Brown eyes like the brown in a child's first paintbox. Wire-framed spectacles. He's been in several institutions for alcohol and drug abuse, but has been rehabilitated for a few years.

On the way they stop at a farm stall-cum-play park. There are swings for children and animals in cages. In one of the cages, in a small hammock, is a bad-tempered monkey. He has white fluff on the sides of his small black face and regards them malevolently. They buy aniseed rusks and farm eggs.

Jameson Bay is bigger than Magrieta expected, but they decide to explore the place properly the next day. She had hoped their self-catering guesthouse would be on the seafront (she feels the need for the soothing effect of waves), but no, it seems they were misinformed, because they have to follow a winding track, higher and higher up against the low, mountainous hill, past a few holiday homes, spaced far from one another, to a few guesthouses planted in a row at the summit – apparently a new extension. From here they look down on a wide, deserted plain. Far below them lies the town; the sea is barely visible from here. In front of each guesthouse is a rusty fishing boat, planted with cacti. For the rest, sun-blanched shells on the ground. They arrive in the late afternoon – the white shells reflect the light, everything is radiantly white and overexposed, an onslaught on the eye, and the wind is blowing.

The guesthouse has two small bedrooms, a living area and a stoep. Magrieta and Isabel share one of the rooms. The place has a seaside theme (to compensate for the fact that there's only a glimpse of the sea at this distance). Every possible surface is decorated with shells, bedside lamps in the shape of lighthouses, a large painted seascape on the wall, seagulls, seaweed motifs, crabs, driftwood, anchors, rope, glass starfish in deep red, dark blue and sea green. The colours are turquoise and white, with a touch of oxblood here and there.

When the sun sets on that gigantic plain, the whole expanse is bathed in a warm light. All the objects in the garden in front of the guesthouse and in the vicinity dissolve in the hazy glow. Still too much light, too sharp. Cool indoors. A coolness that threatens to enfold Magrieta like bat wings. Too light outside, too cool inside, and the merciless wind.

Isabel makes food. With her long fingers she distractedly shreds the lettuce into small, bite-sized strips. Her iPod is propped into her ears and she moves rhythmically to the music. She's making a niçoise salad; she boils eggs, she opens the can of tuna. She slices the tomato and the onion. They sit down to eat. The wind is still blowing unabated.

She says the smell of eggs gives her the creeps. Everything gives her the creeps, actually. Everything smells bad to her, she thinks she has an overdeveloped sense of smell. It's a nuisance.

'If I'd had a cloaca like a chicken,' she says, 'I'd have killed myself.'

'Well, fortunately you don't,' says Magrieta.

'Yes,' says the girl, 'fortunately, it's bad enough as it is.'

Jakob looks at her with interest, but offers no comment.

Magrieta tells them about Deneys Swiegers' mechanical duck (as she calls it). Why a duck? Isabel asks. She wouldn't know, Magrieta says, she assumes Swiegers likes ducks.

It reminds her of the silver swan automaton from the eighteenth century driven by clockwork, Isabel says. It can move its head back and forth, preen its feathers, and bend down to catch a fish from the stream on which it's floating. No, says Magrieta, she knows about the swan, Swiegers' duck is much more lifelike – it's a soft robot, its control system based on the principles of neural networks. And it's much smaller.

After the meal they sit companionably in the living area, reading. Isabel is reading *American Gods*. She doesn't have a very developed taste in reading, she says. Jakob is reading a small Argentinian novella. It's based on a moment in the life of the nineteenth-century German artist Johann Moritz Rugendas, a brief and dramatic incident in the Argentinian pampas that interrupts his travels and brands him for the rest of his life. He likes it a *lot*, he says. It's his kind of book. It's given him an idea for the novel he's struggling with at the moment.

By the time she goes to bed that evening, Magrieta has heard nothing from Potsdam about the person she is here to meet. She's anxious, but ascribes it to the mercilessly raging wind.

*

In the course of the night Magrieta gets up to go to the toilet. She must be groggy with sleep, because she loses her balance and slips on the shower mat. She lands on her coccyx. The pain and shock cause her to lose control of her bladder. She tries to get up, but can't move. She tries to drag herself forward.

'Aaah,' she hears herself moan, 'aaah.'

She calls out. Isabel comes rushing from their room. She tries to lift Magrieta, but battles. Jakob also emerges, bewildered and myopic (half-blind). The girl says to him: 'Put your glasses on and help me.' She is spectrally beautiful by moonlight.

'Aaah,' Magrieta moans, 'aaah.'

Vaguely she registers that the wind has stopped blowing. They help Magrieta onto her bed. Ice, says the girl. But there is no ice. And besides, the pain is deep inside her body, where the coccyx curves inwards. Isabel commands Magrieta to lie on her side. She rolls a towel up tightly and presses it against her coccyx. The pressure brings some relief. She gives her two Panados. See if you can sleep, she says. We'll call the doctor first thing tomorrow.

The next morning Isabel finds the name of the town doctor on a list of emergency numbers. She drives, because Magrieta can't move her legs without pain. Jakob is in a state of panic. He once said to Magrieta that he likes adventure, but he's not much use in a crisis. His bandana is skew, his stubble is unshaven, his face is contorted, his eyeballs are jittering. You'd swear *he* was the injured party, Magrieta thinks through the haze of pain.

The wind had started blowing again in the early morning.

In the car on the way, Magrieta receives an SMS from Markus Potsdam: *The person will contact you tomorrow.*

What, she thinks, this is no time to meet agents!

'Aaah,' she moans with pain when she gets out of the car, 'aaah.'

The girl is ashen, she and Jakob support Magrieta, one to an arm, all the way into the waiting room. The doctor's consulting room is in his house. His assistant is short and solid, with an enormous, towering head of hair and black-framed glasses. Nana Mouskouri gone wrong, Magrieta thinks, and groans. Her class teacher in grade two had the same hairstyle, exactly such a teased hairdo sprayed rock-hard with hairspray. The doctor's consulting room is dark and cluttered; on the wall are antelope heads, on the floor are animal skins and stacked cardboard boxes. The room smells musty like a museum. A big-game hunter and hoarder. Between spasms of pain Magrieta wonders how hygienic such a chaotic and fusty consulting room can be.

After he's palpated her coccyx and examined her, the doctor gives her an injection for pain and a muscle relaxant. He administers it in the soft flesh of her buttock, near the coccyx. His touch is indeed that of a hunter – Magrieta's gluteal muscle quivers like the nervous flank of an animal, struck by an arrow, when the needle pierces the skin. It stings like hell. The moment she sits down at his desk again, nausea overwhelms her. The blood drains from her face and she starts sweating. The assistant brings a bowl into which Magrieta can vomit and a wet cloth with which to wipe her face. Magrieta stumbles out of the consulting room with two packets of pills and the wet cloth pressed to her forehead. Isabel and Jakob are instantly at hand to support her as far as the car. The wind is blowing more fiercely than ever. The car battles against the wind up the low mountain. Magrieta groans with pain and nausea. When they get out at the guesthouse, a new wave of nausea assaults her. Isabel nimbly turns her so the wind doesn't blow Magrieta's vomit back onto her.

The injection must have been strong; she lies down on a divan in the living area and immediately falls into a deep and dreamless sleep. She must have slept for three hours non-stop. Willem is on a business trip to Johannesburg, she decides not to phone him – it would just upset him and there's nothing he can do about her condition.

The rest of the day she spends in a coma on the divan. Isabel brings tea, she makes food. In her woozy state Magrieta hears scraps of their conversation, she registers that the wind is still blowing. By afternoon the injection must have worn off, because she has a headache and her coccyx aches. She takes more pain pills and a muscle relaxant. She is not in a good frame of mind. Here the three of them are, waiting for information and instruction from Markus Potsdam, and she can hardly clench her fists.

The next morning she feels shaky and unstable on her feet, but well enough to get up. Isabel suggests that they go for a walk, it could only benefit Magrieta to move around. They walk slowly along the dirt road. The wind has died down a little. Low shrubs – juniper-green fynbos, darker olive-green shrubs and something grey – everything shivering lightly in the breeze. The soil is dark red. The surrounding mountainous hills are blackened by fire, and descend steeply to the town below; small footpaths criss-cross them like scars. Not a tree in sight. From one point the sea is visible. Far below them is the bay. The sea is one great shiny expanse all the way to the horizon.

The previous afternoon there had been an SMS from Potsdam, she sees: *There has been a delay. The person will contact you later.*

She doesn't feel up to replying to him or informing him about her condition.

That afternoon they go to have fish and chips in the village. The little shop is in the harbour complex, among low, factory-like buildings. Behind the counter, women with nets over their hair, who look more like housewives than workers, prepare the fish and chips. The place is heavily patronised, people wait patiently for their orders. When they are given their food, the three of them sit in the car; there doesn't seem to be anywhere with a view where they can sit on a bench or under a tree. No sign of the sea. They look straight into a brick wall. Everything around them is brick and concrete, which reflects the heat back remorselessly. No shade, no tree in the immediate vicinity, they sit in the hot car, wordless, and ingest the greasy fish and chips, occupied with their own thoughts. Magrieta's are shallow, focused on her pain and physical discomfort, her affected vision. (All objects look one-dimensional, as if observed from a great distance, out of the corner of her eye.)

On their way home they see a crowd of people on the beach. Isabel says they should go and see what's happening. When they stop, they see the beached whale.

'Fuck a buck,' says Isabel.

'It's Jonah's fish,' says Magrieta, stunned.

They walk up closer. A humpback whale, she sees. A remarkably big one. (Magrieta knows her mammals, she is not acquainted with worms alone.) A huddle of people are massed around the dead fish.

How still the great animal lies. Its long pectoral fins are stretched out flat. The shallow wavelets lap against its great ridged tail. The creature is dark, with characteristic white patches – the pattern of each animal as distinctive as fingerprints. The ventral grooves under its jaw are clearly visible.

The wind, still blowing a gale this morning, has since died down. The sea is as smooth as a mirror. There is not a cloud in the sky.

A dead silence descends. A silence as if under a bell jar. Magrieta gazes with awe and wonderment at the dead creature. She walks around him slowly, very slowly. She looks into the milky, unseeing eye. So different from the human eye. So poignantly embedded in the protective ocular folds. She lays her hand carefully on the gigantic flank. How still the leviathan from the depths lies now. Until so recently, he must have experienced so many of the wonders of the depths. He must have sung and breached, ecstatic, and sank back in. Now he is an inert mass. He must have navigated the Arctic Seas, the warmer subtropical waters too. He must have seen the monstrous fish on the ocean floor, braved schools of killer whales and other dangers. He must have covered immense distances, this exuberant fish – the most exuberant of all fish.

She thinks of Jonah who washed up on the shore, after three days in the belly of the fish. His mouth full of sand, his clothes bleached by the animal's potent stomach juices; covered in slime, new as a newborn, blinking against the sharp sunlight. She suddenly thinks, with shocking clarity, of the three leviathan messages behind three toilet doors. Every time in black koki pen.

Magrieta is overwhelmed. She is deeply moved by the presence of the gigantic apparition from the depths. The leviathan. In her half-drugged state, still high on painkillers and anti-inflammatories (the doctor prescribed too high a dose, but this she does not know), the fish could be a vision looming up before her. The fish a vision and the koki messages a sign.

In her head she feels a small shift, like two tectonic plates sliding over each other.

Some of the bystanders are taking selfies in front of the animal, but Magrieta wants to fall to her knees and say: I HAVE HEARD! I TAKE NOTE! I AM MINDFUL!

She trembles. Her legs are weak and her eyes feel teary. Isabel takes her arm and asks if she's okay. Yes, Magrieta murmurs, I'm okay. (But she doesn't know if she really is – complex emotions have taken possession of her. Her heart beats violently in her chest.) Let's go, says Isabel. (She has a handkerchief pressed to her nose – the overdeveloped sense of smell.) Jakob is standing sheepishly at a distance. It looks as if he's also moved, or just embarrassed.

'Are you okay?' the girl asks again, concerned, and takes Magrieta by the arm. She nods. She allows herself to be led away. But in the car she instantly regrets not having stayed longer.

Magrieta lies with her head lolling against the back rest. Her right eye wanders, a sign of too much emotion. She talks at random, incoherently, about the whale. The eye as big as a grapefruit. An inquisitive eye, observers allege. To be confronted eye to eye underwater with the living fish! The eye was extinguished today. A strange unseeing membrane over it. To make you weep. The hide is apparently exceedingly sensitive. A tremor ripples through the huge body when it is stroked even with the fingertips. Imagine that. And with an unusual sheen. Like that of no other animal. Must be the oil secretion. The humpback is a baleen whale. Family Balaenopteridae, genus *Megaptera*. That means giant wings. The males sing complex songs. Of all the whale species they have the longest pectoral fins. They are also the loudest and most inquisitive of all whales.

Isabel and Jakob are sitting silently in the front of the car. Every now and then, Isabel checks in the rear-view mirror that Magrieta is still okay.

She is not okay. She feels terrible. When they get back to the guesthouse, she lies down on the divan in the living area again (the bedroom just freaks her out even more). On her back she feels the least pain. All afternoon she is restless and nauseous, with a massive, threatening headache that she only just keeps at bay with the pain pills the doctor gave her. The wind has come up again and is howling around the corners of the house. It howls across the great, empty expanse below them where nothing checks it – neither tree nor house, neither ditch nor hillock.

She receives an SMS from Markus Potsdam: *Meet the person tomorrow morning at the harbour.*

She SMSes back: *I slipped and fell. Don't expect anything from the meeting.*

Isabel suggests going back home early the next morning – Magrieta is clearly not feeling well. They should have left yesterday, actually. Markus Potsdam will have to come to a different arrangement with his Agent So-and-So. They might as well stay, says Magrieta, they're here now. She wants to go and look at the leviathan again anyway.

The sun sets. All the world is bathed in light. They eat something. Magrieta is high and incoherent. Please, she wants to go back to look at the fish again. They must go back immediately. It's still light enough. It's unworthy for such a magnificent animal to be washed up like that. But it's a sign. She thinks it's a sign. She has to go and look. She's had advance warning. There were three messages on the back of toilet doors in three different places. In black koki pen. She can't disregard it. They must please return to the beach *immediately*. Something is going on here. (The girl looks at her askance and Jakob looks really alarmed. He blinks his eyes and keeps jabbing his glasses back onto his nose.)

The girl placates her. Maybe it's not a good time. Maybe they've hauled the dead animal away already.

The sun has almost set when they drive down to the beach after all. There is a cluster of people and a few police cars where the fish lay washed up earlier. The carcass was indeed removed this afternoon – a bulldozer hauled it away, a policeman informs her. A bulldozer, how dreadful, Magrieta exclaims. Upset, she asks where it was taken. He doesn't know, a dumping site, he thinks. She doesn't take this news well either – she wrings her hands, laments a little.

Isabel takes her arm firmly. They walk to where the people are huddled together. On the sand, in the deep trench left by the dragged-away whale, lies a person covered in a blanket. It seems a couple going for a beach walk had come across the body a little while earlier. They don't know what the person died of, there was a lot of blood. The woman is hysterical. She cries, the man explains something to the police, who have already arrived on the scene.

The wind is still blowing, it blows fine grains of sand against their legs. The sea is stormy, different from this morning, the breakers are noisy. A mist is rising over the sea. The lights of the police cars are flashing. The police are trying to chivvy the bystanders away from the crime scene. Magrieta feels nauseous, the shape under the blanket with a dark bloodstain in the sand above its head is not a pleasant sight; she is highly upset about the leviathan that has been hauled off. (What is a dumping site?) In her dazed condition she tries to make connections between the signs behind the three toilet doors, the fish and the murdered person. Is there a connection, are these things related, are there clues that she's missing?

The van from the Salt River morgue also turns up. Photos are taken of the crime scene. They have to be quick, because the tide is coming in.

Isabel, who still has a firm grip on Magrieta's arm, says, come, we're going, there's nothing more for us here. But Magrieta insists on staying until the body has been loaded onto a gurney and slid into the back of the vehicle. Soon, all tracks and signs of the fish will have been obliterated by the incoming tide, and everything will be as if it never happened. All clues will have been destroyed.

Once again they make their way in the car up the low mountain in the howling wind. Isabel makes tea. She makes them sandwiches. Jakob is visibly disturbed and Magrieta is rattled.

She wants to know if there is such a book as Jonah in the Bible; she can suddenly not remember.

'Jonah comes between Obadiah and Micah,' says Jakob.

Is she remembering the story correctly, Magrieta wants to know. First Jonah gets a message from God. He has to go and cry against the people for their wickedness.

'The great city of Nineveh, he must go to Nineveh,' says Jakob. 'He buys a ticket at the harbour Joppa. He hopes to flee from the presence of the Lord by sailing to Tarshish.'

'Why does he want to flee from the presence of the Lord?' asks Isabel. Sorry, she says, her parents aren't religious, so she's not familiar with the Bible. But she realises it's an important point of reference that she lacks. That and poetry.

'Nineveh was an Assyrian city,' says Jakob, 'and is close to the present-day city of Mosul in Iraq. Then there's a storm at sea. The sailors cast off the cargo to lighten the ship, but Jonah had gone to sleep in the cargo hold.'

'Whatever for?' Isabel asks.

Magrieta is lying with her eyes shut, her head against the back of the chair. Her feet feel very far from her head. Her coccyx is throbbing. 'Probably to flee even further from the presence of the Lord.'

'Makes sense,' says Isabel.

'Then the captain woke him and said he had to pray to his god,' says

Jakob. 'Then the sailors cast lots to see who caused the storm. It fell on Jonah. So he said he was a Hebrew and that he was fleeing from the presence of God. Then the storm got worse. Jonah said they should throw him into the sea, he was the cause of the storm. At first they didn't want to, they didn't want his death on their heads, but then they threw him into the sea. Then the storm calmed immediately. God then sent a fish to swallow Jonah. In the belly of the fish Jonah prayed and promised to execute God's command. Then God ordered the fish to spit Jonah out.'

'After three days,' Magrieta murmurs. 'And three nights.'

How does Jakob come to know the story so well? asks Isabel.

He reread the Old Testament last December, he says. Last year great parts of the wall of Nineveh were destroyed by ISIS, and the tomb of Jonah in Mosul was blown up by them about two years ago.

'Pigs,' Magrieta murmurs, 'fundamentalist pigs.'

She is still not ready to let go of the fish. She is nauseous. Her head feels big and hot. Her throbbing coccyx feels badly bruised. The soles of her feet are burning, but her bones feel cold. She's afraid to go to sleep, afraid of what the night might bring in the shape of terrifying dreams and visions. She feels an aversion to everything here, all the ludicrous gewgaws and knick-knacks – the shells, the bedside lamps, the seascape on the wall, the glass starfish, the colours, the textures; she mustn't even *think* about the aniseed rusks, and she has no desire for tea. She thinks the howling wind may yet drive her mad tonight.

What else do they know about the leviathan? she demands.

In the Middle Ages the Leviathan was an image of Satan, says Jakob, who wanted to devour the creatures of God. Thomas Aquinas describes it as the demon of envy. The Leviathan is depicted on cathedral portals and in illuminated manuscripts as the gaping jaws of hell, the Hell-mouth, the monstrous animal into whose jaws the damned disappear at the Last Judgment.

Magrieta has cramps, like tiny electric shocks, in her legs. Her head feels as if it's not part of her body. As if she could pick it up and put it down elsewhere.

The girl's abundant head of hair is tied back in a ponytail and on her otherwise pale face there is a slight flush – she won't let on, but the events of the past few hours have upset her as well.

'A footnote to Jonah in the Revised Standard Version of the Bible says that the Leviathan refers to a crocodile, also that in the Old Testament it refers to a hippopotamus,' says Jakob.

'There the Bible is spot-on,' Magrieta murmurs, 'because genetically the whale is the closest relative of the hippopotamus.'

He's not quite sure of his facts, says Jakob, but he once read that in Jewish literature, the Leviathan – and especially its eyes – was said to be possessed of great illuminating power.

Magrieta closes her eyes. She is still lying with her head against the back rest of the chair. Her coccyx aches. Her head aches. She is nauseous. She is dizzy. She says she can understand why it was believed that a great illuminating power could come forth from the leviathan. She experienced something of that today in the presence of that beached animal, and the animal wasn't even alive any more. It breaks her heart that the experience was so short-lived. As does the thought that that noble denizen of the deep sea – whether identified with Satan in the Middle Ages, or whenever by whoever, or not – should have ended up in a dumping site.

But now she's on again about the three leviathan messages in black koki pen she discovered behind three different toilet doors. She is certain it was a sign. Of what she doesn't yet know, but how could it, in conjunction with the appearance of the dead fish, be anything other than a message?

Well, suggests the girl tactfully, it could also just be coincidence. But Magrieta shakes her head firmly, no, she's certain it's more than coincidence.

That night she sleeps restlessly. In the early morning an SMS from

Markus Potsdam wakes her up. *The meeting is off. The person died last night. Sorry for your trouble.*

I would put my head on a block, she tells Isabel and Jakob, that the dead man under the blanket last night was none other than the agent that we were to meet here.

Jakob seems surprised at the statement, but Isabel regards her phlegmatically, without comment.

Back at home Magrieta finds a small item in the newspaper stating that the body of a man was found the previous day on the beach at Jameson Bay, in the same place where a humpback whale was beached earlier in the day. He had succumbed to several stab wounds. His identity has not yet been confirmed.

*

Back home, increasingly nauseous and plagued by the most excruciating headaches that none of the doctor's pills relieved, Magrieta consults her own family doctor; she is informed that the doctor in Jameson Bay prescribed far too heavy a dose. In a case like hers the combination of the headache pills and the anti-inflammatories could even have proved fatal. So much then for the big-game hunter's medical prowess. Quack.

On top of it all she suffers severe withdrawal symptoms when she stops taking the pills. For a week she regards the world with a dark and empty eye. Nothing is good, and she takes no delight in anything.

One morning at this time, disgruntled and morose, she asks Potsdam point-blank why he is always so secretive about everything. And why refer to associates as agents? Is it pure chance that the word smacks of espionage? The man they had to meet in Jameson Bay, for instance. The one who by chance just suddenly died. Without any further explanation. What is she to make of it? What was wrong with him, under what circumstances did he die? Everything swept under the carpet, as she is sure so many other things have been, things they don't even know about, because Potsdam doesn't take the trouble to communicate properly with them.

She stops talking. He looks up. She is startled by his expression – so tight-lipped, so uncommunicative she has never seen him. He's not looking well, she realises, his eyes are red and he is unshaven. (A weekend of debauchery and drinking behind him?) His thick eyelashes seem even more incongruous than usual this morning on his pale, bearded face.

'Is there anything else, Magrieta?' he asks.

'Yes,' she says. 'I want to know how the man we were supposed to meet in Jameson Bay – another one of your so-called agents – died.'

'I am a busy man, Magrieta,' he says. 'Say what you want to say and keep it brief. The man was asthmatic. He died in his hotel room in Cape Town.'

'And what was I supposed to find out or negotiate with the asthmatic agent?'

'That is no longer of any importance.'

'You don't say,' she says.

He doesn't react. Carries on with what he's doing on his computer.

'Be that as it may, I want to know what you're involved with, because if it's anything that's not completely kosher, I don't want to be part of it.'

'Magrieta,' he says, 'if the work is not to your liking, say so. If you suspect me of all kinds of dishonest dealings, I suggest you seek your fortune elsewhere. I have little time for paranoia.'

Reprimanded, upset and with burning cheeks, she leaves his office.

When she and Isabel are having lunch in the coffee shop under the Bureau later that day, Magrieta asks her what she thinks of Markus Potsdam, because he acts oddly at times, has a strange management style, and is excessively antisocial, really.

Yes, Potsdam is strange, says the girl. For sure. She's not sure whether he should give her the creeps. Although all strange men give her the creeps, actually. (Magrieta remembers the egg in Jameson Bay that gave Isabel the creeps.)

'I'm actually a creep machine,' she says.

'What is it about strange men that gives you the creeps?' Magrieta asks.

'That they have questionable hygiene. Bodily hygiene, but more specifically their hands – because you have more dealings with their hands than with the rest of their bodies.'

'Do you have any reason to believe that Potsdam doesn't wash his hands?'

'No,' says Isabel. 'No, he actually looks quite clean to me. But I can never be sure.'

'What else gives you the creeps?'

'Well,' says the girl, 'flies give me the creeps. Feet give me the creeps. Human waste gives me the creeps – the merest whiff makes me gag. Dustbins give me the creeps. Any food on my or anybody else's hands – but especially raw meat. Eating utensils that aren't totally clean give me the creeps. Dirty laundry gives me the creeps. Towels and dishcloths. Especially towels in public toilets. Floors, especially rough concrete floors when I'm barefoot. Metal against my teeth, and any other metal scraping against something, because it reminds me of the feeling of metal against my teeth.'

'Then I suppose earthworms will also give you the creeps,' says Magrieta.

'No, not really. I will wash my hands after touching an earthworm. But it's more about the earth than the worm.'

'I have to laugh,' says Magrieta.

'That's okay,' says the girl, 'I suppose it *is* a bit crazy.'

'I suppose open wounds give you the creeps?'

'No, but when I see an open wound I get an empathic pain in my left shoulder.'

'Okay,' says Magrieta, 'interesting, but to get back to Potsdam. In what way do *you* find him strange?'

'He *does* have an unconventional management style,' says Isabel, 'and he *is* very uncommunicative, but he's solid. I've googled him. I checked out his CV and his career thoroughly. Solid credentials. Star performer at school. Star performer at university. Brilliant student. To Oxford as a Rhodes scholar. But apparently he interrupted his promising academic career quite suddenly to return to South Africa.'

'Where he now . . .' says Magrieta.

'Runs a small-time bureau,' says the girl.

'Yes. But what did he do in the years between getting back from Oxford and now?'

'That's the point,' says Isabel. 'He did several different things. Very diverse. Managed a Spar in Nelspruit. Started up an Internet firm in Midrand. Started a financial weekly. For instance. But there are gaps. And the various things are just too diverse. Makes a girl think.'

'It doesn't sound good,' says Magrieta.

'No,' says the girl, 'something doesn't add up. Why hop like that from one thing to the next?'

'A tragic flaw in his character, maybe,' says Magrieta. 'A fault line. Or an Achilles heel?'

'For instance. But I have a hunch there's something here that we're not seeing. He must have some kind of problem. He starts something, then he drops it. If it's a tragic flaw, it's not readily apparent.'

'Drink?'

'No, not drink, and not drugs either.'

'How do you know that with such certainty?'

'Trust me, I know,' says the girl. 'I know the signs.' (Magrieta leaves it there for the time being, she can ask Isabel later how she comes to be so well acquainted with the signs.)

'Gambling, maybe?'

'No. He doesn't have a gambler's profile. But I could always hack his computer. Easy as pie.'

'No,' says Magrieta, 'absolutely not. Under no circumstances. If we start doing that . . . no.'

'Okay, if you say so.'

'An aberration,' says Magrieta. 'A dangerous leaning towards darkness maybe, something that trips him up in every situation?'

'Exactly,' says Isabel. 'I can buy the idea of a leaning towards darkness. Dark energy.'

'What is dark energy?'

'The observable accelerated expansion of the universe is ascribed to it. But we still have no idea what it really is – there's been no directly observable evidence of its existence yet.'

'Wait a minute,' says Magrieta, 'fascinating, but we're getting carried away. We have no grounds for these speculations.'

'So what?' says the girl.

'Let's not make all sorts of wild assumptions. They don't lead anywhere.'

'What do you think he does all day on his computer?' asks Isabel.

'I don't know. Bureau administration?'

'You wish. You and I do that. Haven't you noticed that you're doing more and more?'

'Ye-es? Well?'

'We run the Bureau. Potsdam sits at his computer all day and plays sudoku.'

'How do you know that?'

'I looked when he left his office for a moment.'

'Did you spy on him? Isabel, have you hacked his computer already?'

'No! No, I promise you, I haven't. Even though I wanted to.'

'Promise me you won't do it,' says Magrieta. 'It just doesn't feel right. Potsdam is an honourable man. He's odd, but he's honourable. That's my gut feeling. I like him, even though he's so curt that sometimes you can't get a fucking thing out of him.'

'Even though he runs this place like an espionage outfit, according to you?'

'That's just a way of putting it,' says Magrieta.

'Personally,' says the girl, 'I want to get out of here as soon as possible, and I suggest you do the same. I'm just waiting for my bursary to be approved.'

'You can't leave me here!' Magrieta exclaims, suddenly alarmed. (What she means is – I like you, you're my only ally in this place with this strange man, I have no other prospects at the moment, and my state of mind is not what it should be.)

'You should start looking out for something else.'

'But I got a hell of a big bonus in December!'

'Whatever. But wait until the dark energy kicks in again. Then we'll see our arses. Sure as eggs.'

'No, wait,' says Magrieta. 'Cut the jokes. Next thing we'll convince ourselves with all these wild assumptions. We know absolutely nothing about the man and we have no proof of anything.'

'Okay,' says the girl, 'you're right. But it remains the case that we're doing more and more.'

'Yes,' says Magrieta, 'yes, I'm afraid that *is* so.'

'And that his office is very empty and very clean.'

'That's true.'

'And that we have no idea what's cooking in his head.'

Magrieta nods. 'Why would one have to know?' she asks.

'So that one is prepared if he makes an unexpected move.'

'Like what?'

'That's exactly the point – how must *I* know?'

*

Magrieta and Willem are walking the dog in the late afternoon. Even at this hour it is hot. Willem walks ahead. He talks. She listens with half an ear.

'You are preoccupied,' he says, 'you're not hearing what I'm saying.'

'I have an odd boss,' she says.

'You need to get out of that place,' he says, 'you're wasting your time there.'

'It's not as if I don't know that,' she says.

Seven

February is an unbearably hot and dry month. The drought tormenting the whole country is the worst in human memory. Registering and
admitting new online students and updating associates take up much of
Magrieta and Isabel's time. Their workload had increased so gradually
that she hadn't noticed it herself until Isabel pointed it out to her. Since
they speculated so freely about Markus Potsdam, she's been watching
him more closely than usual when she's with him in the office. Always
in front of the computer, in the empty office, with only a few books on
his bookshelf, the titles of which Magrieta has thus far only been able
to glimpse. If Isabel is right, and he sits there all day playing sudoku,
the whole situation is even odder. She knows nothing about him, and
there's nobody she can find anything out from. Mrs Beetge refused to
say anything and chances are she didn't know anything anyway. But
Magrieta likes him, there is something in him that appeals to her –
his painful embarrassment when he meets her gaze, perhaps, or the
aura of aloneness that envelops him so palpably. Perhaps even just the
way his shirt always strains across his shoulders. And the pleasure she
takes in his unexpected, ironic comments and SMSs. Her heart goes
out to him. She thinks of William Blake: a soul in swaddling bands.

She still at times thinks of the beached whale, but then she recalls
also her abysmal physical state, how strongly and incessantly the wind
had blown, and her aversion ever since to aniseed rusks. The strange
graffiti behind toilet doors she has as good as forgotten; the photo of
the pictogram she has long since wiped from her cellphone.

In March the heat and the drought persist, unremitting. The sun
already sets appreciably earlier in the evenings, but when she and Willem
go walking after seven, the light is still warm on the mountain. In the

vineyards the leaves are starting to change colour. By the middle of the month all the grapes have not been harvested yet, the unpicked grapes are small, soft and sweet.

At the beginning of April, one late afternoon, the vines still changing colour (autumn is late this year), the sun beneficent on her back, the shadows of the pebbles on the ground just, just starting to lengthen, the dog sniffing among the vines, Magrieta picking at one of the last syrupsweet bunches of grapes, her hands sticky with juice, absent-minded – someone emerges, suddenly, from the vineyard behind her, comes to stand in front of her and blocks her way. A woman. Lily-white. Magrieta had not noticed her. She must have approached her at an angle from the vineyard behind her.

She grabs Magrieta by the arm, her face close to hers.

'You must understand,' the woman says, 'what I've been subjected to in the past few months was more than I could cope with on a daily basis.'

The woman is well dressed but dusty and creased, as if she's been sleeping in her clothes. Her hair is unbrushed, slightly flat on one side. Behind her, in the last rays of the setting sun, the mountain turns an eerie kidney- or liver- or blood-pink.

'It felt like everything would come crashing down on my head every day: the never-ending griping about the besieged language, the shit on Afrikaans radio, the words of Afrikaans songs. The news that's read as if the Springbok Top 20's being announced. I couldn't take it any more.'

She gazes ahead, then at Magrieta again.

'I decided to put a tent up for myself in the vineyard.' She gestures in the direction of the vineyard to the left of them. Magrieta looks, but sees no tent. 'My spirit's been in tumult and torment for weeks. Here, in my little tent in the vineyard, is the closest I can get to the wilderness, do you understand?'

Magrieta nods. (Stupefied.)

'Not that I see myself as a kind of self-styled John the Baptist, mind.

Not at all. I'm simply not the locust and wild honey type. I never even read the mystics – Teresa of Ávila and those types. The time had just come for me to isolate myself. The first thing I did was to commit Facebook suicide. It was difficult, believe me, it was very difficult to cut myself free of that addictive web. The second thing was to tell my husband: Go! I'm giving you your freedom. You are now free to make of your life whatever you see fit.'

She gazes in front of her for a moment, turns to Magrieta again, puts her hand on her arm and says: 'Do you understand?' Once again Magrieta nods.

'But the hardest of all,' says the woman, 'was giving up my cellphone. Look, if you think escaping the Facebook web was hard, I'll tell you what hard is. It was *hell* letting my smartphone go! The very latest model. Slim, a triumph of technology, with a staggering number of functions. A beautiful object, perfectly proportioned – beautiful as a classical Grecian urn is beautiful. That was the last thing I cast off from myself. I threw it into the river down there. For a moment I was stunned – what on earth had got into me, I thought. I hesitated, I considered wading into the river to try to retrieve it. God, I thought – there goes my umbilical cord! There goes the one thing that connects me to everything in my life! I stumbled ahead, my arms outstretched like a blind person. It was like entering darkness, it was as if part of me had been torn out. I felt I was being cast back into a kind of medieval darkness of the spirit.'

The woman gazes in front of her. Speechless, Magrieta listens.

'That phone,' she murmurs, 'in the mornings when I woke up, it was the first thing I reached for, only when I felt that familiar shape, the familiar weight of it in my palm, was I ready to tackle the day. In the evenings it was the last thing . . . it was like a limb, a prosthesis, that I strapped on in the morning and took off in the evening. It was like an umbilical cord, a lifeline, keeping me connected to the world. Do you understand?'

Magrieta nods. (She hopes fervently that her phone won't ring at that moment and cast the woman into a panic of bitter remorse.)

'But enough,' says the woman, 'if you'll excuse me. I've talked enough for one day. I want to store the silence in myself like a bee its honey.'

Her eyes suddenly fill with tears. Two great, warm tears trickle down her cheeks and drop into the dust at Magrieta's feet. They both look down and contemplate them.

Then the woman turns abruptly and strides off between two rows of vines. Magrieta watches her go. At a distance she can only just make her out in the gathering dusk. It could be that her pop-up tent is not far from there, but because the vines still have a fair covering of leaves, and there are grasses with white plumes standing high between the tidy rows of vines, Magrieta quickly loses sight of the woman. A tent in the vineyard. A pop-up tent, or one of the expensive Cape Union Mart numbers?

Magrieta – still rattled by the woman's unexpected appearance – calls the dog, who has in the meantime been exploring the paths between the vines on her own.

On the third day after their first encounter, when walking the dog in the late afternoon (she and Willem don't normally walk this route, but recently he's been working late), Magrieta meets the woman for a second time. Once again she comes up to Magrieta from one of the paths between the vines.

Today there is something feverish about her. Her cheeks are flushed and she talks fast. Magrieta wonders if she could be going down with flu or something, from exposure to the cold night air, because although the days are sunny, the evenings are chilly already.

'Are you still okay?' Magrieta asks.

The woman nods. 'Never better,' she says.

'Isn't it very cold at night?' Magrieta asks.

'The tent is warm,' the woman says, 'I'm not cold.'

'You haven't been . . . molested or anything yet?'

The woman shakes her head vehemently, no.

'May I ask,' says Magrieta, 'what made you decide to come here?' and she gestures vaguely in the direction of the vineyard behind them.

'My head was clattering so badly,' says the woman. Behind her the sun is starting to set flame-red. 'And I was starting to suffer from apocalypse fatigue.'

'Apocalypse fatigue?'

'Yes,' says the woman, 'all the end-of-time scenarios: the threat of Islam, ISIS, Boko Haram, asteroids that could collide with the earth any day, the shifting tectonic plates, tsunamis, leaks at nuclear power stations, an unusually large solar flare that could bedevil the electricity supply on earth for 25 years, the threat of robots, treatment-resistant diseases like TB. And that little personal apocalypse: creeping old age.'

The whole western sky is bathed in a golden light.

The woman talks fast, her cheeks glow in the warm light of the setting sun. 'During the day there was a pressure in my head and at night my heart beat uncontrollably. The only thing that afforded relief was buying things, but what I bought gave me no pleasure. What was the beauty of nature to me? Nothing. The mountains? The shifting cloud formations? The magnificent autumn colours? What was *anything* to me – my heart felt like something that had been lying on an ash heap for a long time: a mouldering, half-decomposed, fungus-covered beetroot.'

Yes, Magrieta sees, the autumn colours, the whole autumnal season, are indeed magnificent. It could not but strike her too these past few days. The vineyard practically glows in the waning light. The colours of the leaves – backlit in the last warm rays of the sun – vary from brilliant orange to a deep liver-red, with here and there still a last green accent.

'My husband impeded my inner vision,' the woman says, 'and I his. Look, I'm practically talentless. I have no literary talents and I have no spiritual talents. What is someone like me to do? How do you live your life – without talent and superficially? That is what I started asking myself.'

She comes a step closer to Magrieta. There are tears in her eyes, two hectic spots on her cheeks; she speaks fast: 'My husband has money and status. He no longer appealed to me.' She thumps her heart. 'Not *here*. My children just found me a burden. For a long time they've been better off without my fretful interference. Every time I walked here with the dog, and noticed the holes in the ground, I longed more and more for a return to a torpid foetal existence. I thought how wonderful it must be to crawl into such a hole, to lead a different kind of life – an anonymous, underground life.

'The church pissed me off a long time ago,' she continues. (Magrieta smells something feverish on the woman's breath, something sharp like ammonia.) 'Their bickering about gay issues. Oh please. The Afrikaners can't seem to move on beyond gayness and evolution. Day after day, articles and letters about it in the newspapers. If it's not about banning gays from the church, it's about the unchristian teaching of evolution. They deserve to be wiped off the face of the earth, actually, language, dim-witted convictions and all. And then the dog. In my case a poodle. One of those big ones. I fetch the dog from the salon, coiffed and pomaded. His food costs more than my domestic worker earns in a month. Lies on the back seat. On my way home I bang my fists on the steering wheel in desperation. Says the dog: It's the only life you have, you cunt. I almost roll the car. Did I hear that correctly, is the bloody dog talking to me? I concentrate on the road. Again the dog: What are you going to do about it? About what? I ask over my shoulder. About your miserable life, says the dog. Blow me if I don't say to the dog: It's none of your bloody business. That was the turning point. That afternoon I went and bought myself the tent at Cape Union Mart.'

They are standing close to each other, Magrieta and the woman. She looks up urgently at Magrieta.

'Do you understand?' she asks.

'I understand,' says Magrieta (dumbfounded).

The woman is breathing quickly. Her hair is tangled. 'Do you understand that I no longer actually had a choice?'

Magrieta nods. She wonders all of a sudden whether she shouldn't tell the woman about the leviathan. The woman – clearly in extremis – might perhaps find her unusual experience with the beached fish interesting. But she thinks better of it.

They say goodbye. The woman turns around and walks away quickly along the same path from which she appeared.

When Magrieta walks further with the dog, past a few hollowed-out holes in the path, she suddenly regards them with great interest. She hadn't noticed these holes before. Yes, she thinks, wouldn't it be remarkable indeed to crawl into such a hole.

A week or so later, in mid-April, Magrieta comes across the woman a third time. She is sitting on a large rock next to one of the paths between the vines. She looks even dustier and more crumpled than before; her hair looks even more tangled. She's sitting with a blood-red vine leaf in her hand. The breeze stirs the hem of her dress lightly (the expensive little sand-coloured linen number is looking considerably more threadbare and less fresh than before).

They greet each other.

'How are you?' Magrieta asks. The woman shakes her head slowly from side to side. Closes her eyes for a moment. 'I'm starting to find peace now,' she says.

Today there is no sign of the feverishness. She peers dreamily over Magrieta's shoulder in the direction of Table Mountain – only just visible in the distance.

'What are you going to do when it starts raining?' Magrieta asks. (The drought has not broken yet, neither here nor elsewhere in the country. The first rains of winter have not yet fallen. The days are exceptionally hot and dry. Unusual for this time of year. The woman can count herself lucky.)

'I have a good tent,' she says, 'bought down in the town from Cape Union Mart, as I've mentioned.' (Must have cost the earth, Magrieta thinks.)

'Do you have enough to eat?'

'I have enough.'

'Aren't you scared of the dark?'

'No more scared than I was at night in my suburban house in my suburban bed. I had to get away, even if it means I perish or am wiped out here.'

'What about undesirable elements here in the vineyard?' Magrieta asks.

She shrugs. 'If it must be, it must.'

Magrieta nods. The woman reflects for a few moments.

'Look,' she says, 'you need to understand. I just wanted to disappear from my life, actually. Not from life *itself*, take note, but from my own, familiar life. I wanted to escape the constant, narcissistic need for gratification, so thoroughly sustained by everything and everybody with which I surrounded myself and in which I saw myself mirrored and reflected. I did not want to give up my life, you understand, I wanted to give up the *self*, the terribly demanding me.'

'That makes sense,' Magrieta murmurs.

They say goodbye and Magrieta walks back.

During the day she executes Markus Potsdam's – increasingly time-consuming and frustrating – directives. In the late afternoon she rushes to the spot in the vineyard where she encountered the woman, every day in the hope of coming across her again. Willem is away, at the bedside of his ailing mother. Magrieta is pleased that she started to take this route by chance, with Willem they'd probably have walked a different way. She fine-combs the newspaper for a possible report on a missing woman, but she finds nothing about this anywhere.

Magrieta encounters the woman four more times. The last time just after the penetrating winter rains have set in, which will prevent Magrieta from going for regular late-afternoon walks. It's an exceptionally unstable time. In spite of the rain the drought has still not broken. Never before have there been so many mountain fires. (Often the work of delinquents and arsonists.) In some towns there is no water. There are riots and demonstrations about service delivery everywhere – burning tyres in the streets, stones thrown at motorists. Schools and factories are burnt down, buses are torched. There are taxi wars and gang violence. Students demonstrate about tuition fees. Statues are vandalised. The continuing drought, the weak economy, the dissatisfaction with local municipalities and corrupt government functionaries all contribute to the tide of unrest and uprising washing over the country.

The woman is more threadbare every time. In the course of their fourth meeting she talks about motherhood. 'Motherhood,' she says, 'is a terrible fate, for the mother, but especially for the child. It does the child irreparable damage. In truth the child should be removed as early as possible from the toxic atmosphere of the mother. The child must be fed and cared for, but left free – away from the short-sighted possessiveness of the mother. Look,' she says, and comes a step closer to Magrieta, as two big tears well up in her eyes, 'I have shed more tears over my children than over the destiny of the entire human race. I bled from the heart for my children, from my spleen, as the poet says, from every one of my organs. Their pain was my pain. But my pity for them, my blind desire to protect them, to want only the best for them, damaged them.'

Magrieta listens to her in horror, she is startled by the woman's words. She is the mother of a child herself, a daughter, now far from here, in another country.

The surrounding vineyards, the great and godly mountains, the splendid celestial dome, the looping bats at dusk, the calling plovers and skittish owls, the changing cloud spectacle by day, the deep fragrance emanating from the earth by night: this is the background against which Magrieta encounters the woman during her late-afternoon, early-evening walks.

And the homeless, Magrieta wonders, those of whom there are traces and signs everywhere: a burnt-out fire here, a charred chicken bone there, a pool of vomit, bloodstains, human excrement, discarded articles of clothing. The vagrant groups with whom the woman shares these surroundings – these divine surroundings – have they already targeted her? The expensive running shoes, the stockpiled food? Will they have already taken note of the white woman – the desirable, rain-resistant tent, the warm clothes, the expensive sleeping bag? Will they already have their eye on her, be planning something for her? Or would they recognise her as one of them, as one of the wretched, those who have nothing, nothing to keep and nothing to lose. Would they embrace her, share their fires and their meagre food with her (a chicken bone and a morsel of bread, a sip of box wine); would she already have adopted a pared-down vocabulary, stripped to the essentials (the secret argot of the poes)? Is that not in any case what the woman was aiming for – renunciation and attenuation? Magrieta worries, and studies the news-paper every day for any possible report of a missing – in the worst case, a murdered – woman. In the paper she does read of a child in the town who was raped by a family member, of shelters burnt down, burglaries, a section of the vineyard that was hacked out for firewood.

Between the fourth and fifth encounters Magrieta has to liaise with several people (agents) in the Peninsula and surrounds. For a few days she has no time to walk the dog in the afternoon. She doesn't think of the woman. Her attention is occupied by the people she has to contact.

But back in town, at the beginning of May, on the very first after-noon, she hurries back to the vineyard. It has rained once in the mean-time. Has the woman survived? Has her tent not been washed away? She comes across her once more sitting on the big rock, in the last warmth of the late-afternoon sun. (Magrieta is relieved.)

She doesn't look good – unwashed and visibly thinner. Today she's wearing old tracksuit pants and a washed-out, home-knit jersey that she folds closer around her thin body. Her lips look chapped, her hair is caked, and is Magrieta imagining it, or is there the shadow of a bruise on one of her cheeks?

'Did the rain not bother you? Aren't you cold at night?' Magrieta asks, concerned.

'No,' says the woman, taken aback, 'my tent is warm. I heard the rain all night long. It sounded different from what rain had ever sounded like before. It's the first time I've ever really heard what rain sounds like. I was a bit cold, but it no longer bothers me that much – cold or heat,' she shrugs, 'cold or heat, that no longer bothers me all that much. It's all *here*,' she says, tapping her head lightly.

'Have you got enough to eat?' Magrieta asks.

'Yes,' says the woman. 'Yes. Look,' she says, touching the worn tracksuit bottom, the jersey, 'I bartered this. I bartered it for bread.'

'From whom?' asks Magrieta, with a sinking feeling, a premonition of disaster.

'From my fellow human being.'

The woman stares dreamily in front of her. 'Do you know,' she says, 'initially my dreams here were confused, chaotic. Now they're getting clearer by the day. It's as if the pool on which I'm drawing is bigger than before. Do you know,' she says, 'the figures in my dreams, they were at first almost like visitations. Like spirits . . . At first I was scared, I was anxious at night, in the dark, but now I realise . . .' She falls silent.

Magrieta waits. 'What do you realise now?' she asks softly. The woman looks at her as if only just registering her presence again.

'Now I realise,' she says, 'that what I thought were visitations . . . don't come from outside, they are the emanations of my own spirit.'

She is talking more slowly, Magrieta notes, more hesitantly.

'Figures . . . women . . . came to me in my dreams,' she says, 'like nothing I'd ever seen before.'

She is silent for a while.

'I saw a woman . . . a red woman came to me, a black woman . . . they smiled . . . one was rocking a dead child in her arms.'

She falls silent again.

'I wasn't scared, strangely enough. I realised that they were the shapes and figures of our earthly existence. The dead child was my old self. I felt great compassion for that dead child.'

When Magrieta calls the dog and starts walking home, she wonders if she shouldn't contact the police, if maybe she shouldn't have done so already. She doesn't know whether the woman is still in a state to look after herself. She is now becoming a soft target for thugs, for anybody hanging out in this vineyard – and there must be plenty of them – with evil intent. These are ungodly times. People are hungry. Mercy, human kindness, generosity, sympathy, nobody can count on these any more. One doesn't see much of these in society any more.

At their sixth, and penultimate, meeting, the woman's clothes are threadbare. It looks as if she has mud in her hair. She's not wearing shoes. Her feet are dirty and blue with cold. Her nail polish is chipped. She is holding an autumn leaf in her hand.

'Where are your shoes?' Magrieta asks.

The woman says: 'I bartered them for bread. For water.'

'From whom?' Magrieta asks.

'From my fellow mortals,' the woman answers. 'Do you know,' she says dreamily, 'I looked into the mirror more and more often – to make sure that I was still there. But the more I looked into the mirror, the greater the distance between me and the world became.'

She gazes in front of her for a long time.

'Now it is being gradually annulled,' she says softly, 'that terrible, dishonouring distance.'

She looks up unexpectedly, into Magrieta's eyes.

'I still have a long way to go,' she says. 'I still know it's *me* who's looking at the leaf in my hand. I still know it's *you* who's standing before me. We are still separate – you and I. But the day will come when you and I and the leaf are one and the same thing.'

Oh Lord, Magrieta thinks. Where is this headed?

Shortly thereafter the first real winter rains start falling. For three days it rains so hard that Magrieta can't go walking in the vineyard. What on God's earth is the woman doing in her pop-up tent in this weather? Magrieta wonders. No tent, not even one of Cape Union Mart's fantastic, weatherproof tents, can keep these driving gusts of rain out. And not just the rain, for two nights the wind blows fiercely, howls, drives the rain in furious drifts. And the worm, thinks Magrieta, the worm that flies in this howling storm, seeking the fragrant bed of the rose, has he perhaps found his destination in the woman's state-of-the-art tent, has he made his bed there, and is he destroying the fragile life within with his dark, secret love?

The last time Magrieta sees the woman she's once again sitting on the big rock. She's not looking good. She holds a bunch of shrivelled grapes out to Magrieta.

'Take, eat,' says the woman. 'It's sweet. There's plenty more,' she indicates over her shoulder. 'If you look carefully among the leaves. Late grapes. The sweetest there is.'

Magrieta hesitates. She takes the little bunch, it's warm and sticky, the grapes are small, no longer firm.

'Haven't you been here long enough?' Magrieta asks cautiously. 'The weather's only going to get worse. It looks like you're out of food. It looks like you're dependent on the people here. That could get dangerous.'

The woman regards Magrieta for a long time. Magrieta's words don't seem to register with her.

'Up to now it's all been about *me*,' she says. 'That is going to change now. I'm starting to reach out. That's why you and I are here.'

'Why are you and I here?' Magrieta asks gently.

'To help all incarnate beings on their arduous passage,' says the woman.

That was the last encounter, although Magrieta did not realise it at the time. She never came across the woman again. When Willem returns from Pretoria, where he's been sitting at the bedside of his ailing mother, she asks him to help her go look for the woman. He asks her why she didn't report the matter to the police at the outset. She says she doesn't know. Something prevented her, she doesn't know what.

No sign of the woman or the tent among the vines. She checks the newspaper every day, but never sees a report of a woman missing in the area. No report of anybody being overpowered, attacked or – God forbid – murdered in the neighbouring vineyards. She reports it at long last to the police, but they don't find any trace of a tent, or body, or clothing either. (She doesn't know how thoroughly they searched; they didn't seem very interested in the case. And why should they be? So many children missing every day, so many murders, rapes, crimes.)

What could have happened to the woman? Perhaps she just decided one day, to hell with this exercise, it's not going to bring her any joy. Packed up the expensive tent, called it quits. Or perhaps she was attacked after all – plundered, raped, murdered, her body hidden some-where, buried. The desirable tent whisked away with the victors – the plunderers and rapists. Pitched elsewhere to provide shelter for those huddling against the onslaught of winter wind and rain.

But whenever Magrieta walks in the vineyard, whenever she has the opportunity, when she's not dispatched on some mission or other by Potsdam, at dusk, after an exhausting day's work, and weather permit-ting, she still hurries back to the place where she last encountered the woman, searching for something, a button, a crust of bread, anything, to confirm that the woman had been there, that Magrieta had not hal-lucinated it.

A month or so after she encountered her for the last time, there is a short article in the paper about a woman who was found dead in the vineyard. Magrieta reads with trepidation, but it seems that an old woman, one Maria Stoffels, was found dead in the vineyard on the farm Rodebergen (precisely on Magrieta's walking route, in the same vine-yard where she met the woman). No crime is suspected. Mrs Stoffels presumably succumbed to exposure to the cold when she went gather-ing wood in the early evening.

Eight

Twice Magrieta invites Markus Potsdam to have coffee with her and Isabel at the coffee shop. Both times he has an excuse; indeed he looks quite startled when she asks him. Afterwards she says to Isabel she's giving up now, let the man spend his days in solitude in front of his computer. She can't force him to do anything against his will. Perhaps he has one hell of a life behind the scenes, Isabel says – booze, sex and rock 'n' roll. Unlikely, says Magrieta, it looks more like a bad case of shyness or something, she doesn't know what. Then he shouldn't do this kind of job where he constantly has to deal with people, says Isabel. Well, he doesn't have to do it, says Magrieta, *she*'s had to run after agents from the start. And if she has to lunch with *one* more donor, she'll croak.

'Shame,' says Isabel.

Magrieta says she's grateful Isabel is there, because if she had to work alongside the inexorable Mrs Beetge and the otherworldly Potsdam, as before, she'd have gone off her rocker.

'Fuck a buck,' says the girl.

The Bureau uses Professor Deneys Swiegers of the engineering department to assess whether their mathematics module is up to standard. He is a pleasant man. Broad, open face, calm gaze, traces of the acne of his youth still visible. A smallish man, his head somewhat large in relation to the rest of his body. Difficult to judge his age, he's probably in his early or late forties. He is always courteous, always prepared to explain patiently what he's occupied with. Magrieta likes visiting him in his laboratory; she likes the feeling of that large open space. She's interested in his work with the mechanical duck (as she likes to think of it). She asks him, why a duck and not a human being? He looks at her placidly with his clear eyes. He originally considered making an eel, he says, then he decided on a duck. He likes ducks. Ducks are less complex than human beings, he says, but a great challenge nevertheless. If this experiment succeeds, he'll move on to something more complex.

(A woman with breasts and a fully functioning cunt, Magrieta thinks.)

The duck is about thirty centimetres high. Snow-white. No feathers, but a soft surface. True to life. The wings can lift. The eye has a calculating expression. The beak can open and close. It can respond to simple instructions, when complete it will even be capable of voice recognition. Magrieta says it must have taken a lot of time and skill, and Swiegers says it *is* a big undertaking, but it is also his passion.

Deneys Swiegers has a research assistant, Bertie Oberholzer, a smallish man, but sturdy like a mountaineer in his shorts and boots. She guesses him to be younger than Swiegers. Dark, hairy, bearded; ruddy complexion. Not very friendly. Even the tolerant Swiegers apparently sometimes finds him a thorn in the flesh because Bertie slanders him behind his back (as Swiegers has on occasion remarked with a sigh to Magrieta): implies that he acquires funds illegally, teaches too little, is too unaccommodating of students.

She tells Swiegers about the bionic skate that was built by a group at Harvard, which imitated the movement of its biological equivalent, not by the electrical currents and servomotors of conventional robots, but by means of muscle cells designed to imitate the elegant undulations of the living fish. These rat muscle cells were grown in a culture, pressed onto elastomer sheets that then formed the surface of the roboskate's wings. Tiny, sixteen millimetres long. Amazing! Oh yes, says Swiegers, he knows about it, he used the same soft materials like latex and silicone for the duck as well.

The hairy, ruddy-faced Bertie Oberholzer puts his head around the door, as he apparently always makes a point of doing when she's with Swiegers. Swiegers' presence is urgently required at a meeting, he says. Swiegers says calmly that he has already requested to be excused today.

Swiegers asks her to tell him a little about the Burgess Shale, she mentioned it the other day, he has only the vaguest notion of it. It's in Canada, as he probably knows, she says, and the fossils date from the Middle Cambrian, about 505 million years ago. The fossil beds there occur in a series of shale layers – about 160 metres deep. She tells him of *Opabinia* and *Hallucigenia*. The latter is a strange fossil, she says, it was initially reconstructed upside down. At first it seemed to stand on toothpicks, with a single layer of tentacles on its back – it does look like something that could be hallucinated, really. But new fossils have shown that it actually stands on little legs, and has a row of spiny points on its back. She makes a quick drawing of it on a sheet of paper.

Bertie Oberholzer puts his hairy head around the door again. Does Swiegers have a moment?

He's coming now, says Swiegers, just give him a few minutes.

'*Opabinia regalis*,' says Magrieta, 'has five little eyes like toadstools and a proboscis snout. Also a strange little fossil. But perhaps the most interesting of the Burgess fossils is *Pikaia* from the Middle Cambrian. Small, about five centimetres long. First classified as a worm and later as the first known example of a vertebrate. A landmark in the history of the phylum to which all vertebrates belong. If *Pikaia* hadn't survived the Burgess elimination, *we* wouldn't be here – not shark nor bird nor orangutan.'

Swiegers nods thoughtfully.

'But the so-called Cambrian explosion is a myth, in fact – there was really only an explosion of fossilisability. Most of the Cambrian phyla date back millions of years to the Pre-Cambrian. On dry land,' says Magrieta, 'on the red plains, there was nothing happening yet.'

She tells him that she's looking out for something else, the job at the Bureau is not very satisfying. She tells him about Professor Mogoerane's project in the Soutpansberg and how much she'd like to go there sometime. One of their first finds, as it happens, was a fossil that looks very much like the *Opabinia* from the Middle Cambrian. The same five eyes and proboscis snout. According to him the site is as rich as the Burgess Shale. A first from this era for South Africa. Very exciting.

Bertie Oberholzer puts his ill-tempered, ruddy face around the door and asks Swiegers if he's still busy. Give me a few moments, says Swiegers calmly. It's well-nigh impossible to have a conversation with Swiegers with the Bertie fellow interrupting them all the time.

Wouldn't it be a good idea, says Deneys Swiegers, to get in touch with the professor and to find out what the possibilities are? Any small change could open up other opportunities.

Bertie puts his hairy head around the door *again* and asks even more impatiently when Swiegers will be done. One of the students has been waiting for half an hour already to see him.

Swiegers raises his hand in a placatory gesture.

Magrieta gets up. Thank you, she says, good idea. She will try as soon as possible to get in touch with Professor Mogoerane.

Later that afternoon she phones Mogoerane's office. (She still has the card he gave her that evening, fortunately.) She's not sure what she'll say to him, but she can at least ask him how the excavations are going in any case.

'Professor Mogoerane is gone,' says the person.

Oh, Lord, she thinks, he's dead. He's died of his injuries from the hijacking.

'When did he die?' she asks.

'No,' says the person, 'he didn't die, he left. He is teaching in America now. He accepted a position at the University of Oklahoma.'

'And his project in the Soutpansberg?'

No, says the person. That's come to a standstill. Damn, Magrieta thinks. Damn Mogoerane who cut and run, although probably understandably under the circumstances. For the time being, then, that's the end of *Opabinia* on home ground.

*

That afternoon Magrieta reports to the psychiatrist for her six-monthly evaluation. She still does not feel well, she says. She doesn't know if the latest pills are working. She needs to change her circumstances, but she doesn't get around to it. The medication can only do so much, he says. (Yes, she thinks, don't blame the medication now if you're just a shit psychiatrist.) He can't see that she can do other than benefit from a good therapeutic conversation.

*

That evening the moon rises like a gigantic ball behind the mountains. Difficult to believe it's rock, it looks like a ball of light, a Chinese lantern. Magrieta stands on the stoep and she thinks she may have concentrated on worms for too long.

She suddenly remembers that she left her purse at the office. When she walks into the Bureau she sees a light under Potsdam's door. When she's about to unlock her door, she hears somebody crying in his office. It's Potsdam himself, without a doubt. Her legs go weak with fright, her heart beats wildly against her ribs. Raw sobs. She has seldom in her life, if ever, heard a man cry like that. She stands still, indecisive. Should she go in and find out what's wrong, or try to get away as quickly as possible before he finds out that she's heard him cry like that?

Without collecting her purse she turns around and quietly leaves the Bureau.

Nine

On the recommendation of the psychiatrist Magrieta makes an appointment with a therapist. She goes, but she is sceptical. When the therapist says, let's begin at the beginning, she digs her heels in and her hackles rise. She has no desire to discuss her childhood and everything before and after that with this or any other person. (Definitely not with *this* person, anyway.) She tells him her parents are dead and buried. The harm they did is done, it's over and done with, there is nothing to be done about it any more. They certainly did their best and acted according to their own best insights, and she is sure that they were no better or worse than most other parents. She does not have the inclination, the time or the energy to turn over every stone of her past and examine every tiny exposed worm with a magnifying glass. Half of what happened to her she's forgotten – no, definitely more than half, the vast majority – and the meagre remains have, with the passing years, probably been rewritten to such an extent that they bear hardly any relation to the original experiences.

That does not *matter*, says the therapist, it's not what happened in the past, it's what she makes of it *now*!

But Magrieta does not feel like it. She does not feel like revisiting, with this man, so radiant with therapeutic conviction, the circumstances of her conception, her birth, childhood, her first depressive episode, the misery of her high school career, the heartbreak of her later troubled relationship with her father.

After this first session she does not make another appointment.

*

Her father was a biology teacher who did photography in his spare time. He developed his photos himself in a small room that he'd fitted out for the purpose. Magrieta enjoyed being there with him; she liked the sharp smell of the chemicals, and seeing the image emerging gradually, but she was impatient with the process. Her father was undistractable, although he sometimes laughed at her odd questions and comments. He photographed landscapes in particular – a narrow horizon line with huge masses of cumulus or cirrus clouds. A single copse of trees in a wide landscape. Waterfalls, mountain slopes covered in aloes. When they were small, he took photographs of her and her brother with a small box camera. When they started going down to the Bushveld for their family visits in winter, he always stopped and photographed the aloes. She, her brother and their mother stayed in the car; her mother was impatient for them to be on their way, but even as a young child Magrieta could see that her father really liked moving among the rocks and the aloes with his camera.

At university Magrieta was ashamed of their smallish house in a middle-class neighbourhood. One evening during her first overseas trip (with a bursary on account of her academic prowess), on the market square in Venice, she told an Afrikaans student in a greatcoat, part of a student tour group, that her father was an advocate. To this day she does not know whether he believed her. He said nothing. A slightly overweight young man, not attractive, he listened to her silently with his hands in his coat pockets. She wanted to create the impression that she had unlimited funds, a rich kid on a European trip.

She was travelling with two friends. Two serious young women, who took the educational value of a European trip seriously, and conscientiously visited all the right museums and sights. In Mycenae Magrieta was for the first time seized by a tremendous resistance. The ruins had nothing to say to her. She could hardly put one foot before the other. She dragged herself along in the wake of the other two, with guidebooks diligently in hand. The same happened in Pompeii. She felt not a scrap of enthusiasm or interest in the remains of the devastated city. All that she can remember of the visit years afterwards are the narrow pathways among the ruins, everything the same brown, and her slow-footed aversion. She was resentful of her energetic friends. Only in Florence, when she could explore the city on her own, did she develop a greater enthusiasm. But in the art galleries she still felt little interest. The art treasures of Europe left her cold. Even in the natural history museums she loitered about listlessly. She wanted to hang out in cafés, she wanted to have adventures, explore things on her own.

Magrieta got depressed for the first time when she was fifteen. As a young child she'd been intensely interested in the world around her, but in the course of one winter holiday she became morbidly introspective. On the way back from a family visit, cold, the East Rand winter-arid, the grass yellowing, the trees bare, the sky smoggy, she sat in the back of the car, disgruntled and discontented. She gazed out of the window at the wintry landscape and there was *nothing*, but *nothing*, that she could take any delight in. With agonising intensity she wanted to be in any place other than in her own skin. There were other depressive episodes later, but never again as violent and deracinating as that first one.

Her father is dead. The man who could look at clouds with such pleasure. Who delighted in nature, who knew the names of each plant, shrub and tree. Who liked the silhouettes of trees against the sunrise and sunset. Who collected Weet-Bix cards. Who liked holidays in the game reserve, or the Bushveld, or on the coast. Hat on his head, cigarette in his mouth. (She remembers him in that hat, in his flannels and his sports jacket and his worried face, next to the car, before every journey they undertook.) The person who inspired her love of worms and insects and dogs – indeed the whole of the natural world. He paged through nature guides with Magrieta, taught her the names of plants and animals. He helped her to build an ant garden and a maze for her snails. He built her a special cabinet for her stone and shell collection. He read to her from *The Soul of the White Ant*, *The House of the Four*

Winds and *From Forest and Plain*. He told her jackal-and-wolf stories. He contrived tales of adventurers in Africa – confrontations with quicksand, natives, pygmies. He explained in detail how gorillas built their nests; he taught her a song that cannibals supposedly sang when they danced around their cauldrons with missionaries inside.

On Sunday evenings her father sat on the sofa in the sitting room, reading and annotating the Bible. Magrieta suspects that his doubts deepened and his faith faltered in his later years, although he never said anything about it. Her mother read novels – thick books that were kept in the passage in the wooden bookshelf with glass doors, and from which Magrieta as a child read in secret.

At thirteen she was given a biography of Alexander von Humboldt as a Christmas present from her parents. She enjoyed this very much. She cast an egg in plaster of Paris and tried to carve the skull of an extinct Atures Indian from it. In the back garden the trees were gravid with fruit. They ate fruitcake. One of her aunts had recently learnt to do yoga and stood on her head in the sitting room. That was one of the last Christmastides that Magrieta enjoyed – when she still took pleasure in everything around her, and in everything she did.

What her father and her mother contributed to her own genetic make-up had never really interested Magrieta. Although she believes, like Steven Pinker, that the behaviour of the child is determined less by environment than by genes.

Ten

When Magrieta arrives back at the office after her first, and as far as she's concerned her last, visit to the therapist, an upset Isabel comes to meet her. Potsdam is gone, she says. What does she mean, gone? Magrieta asks. Gone as in there's a note saying we must take the reins, he's sure we'll do it well, he'll be away for a while, he can't say how long, unfortunately.

'Show me the note,' says Magrieta.

Indeed. A short message, addressed to her and Isabel. He's going away, he doesn't know for how long. There is a list of assignments for each of them on their computers. He trusts that there will be no problems.

'Oh, Lord,' Magrieta murmurs.

They go into Potsdam's office. If it had been empty before, it's now doubly empty. At least his presence had always filled the space, after a fashion.

Magrieta is upset. She should have gone in that evening when she heard him crying. She should have forced him to tell her what was wrong.

'It looks a lot like his previous tricks, a few months in one place and then he's gone. How long has he been running this show?' Isabel asks.

'I don't know,' says Magrieta. 'I don't know exactly. I don't even know where he lives! The only place I've ever seen him is in this office at his computer.'

'Playing sudoku,' says Isabel.

'How are we going to get hold of him to find out if he's okay?' She hasn't told Isabel or Willem how Potsdam had been crying here that evening. 'Where do we start?' she asks, panic-stricken. 'Why is his computer still here?'

'His computer is still here because there's nothing of interest left on it. You should have let me hack it when I wanted to,' Isabel comments drily.

'Oh good Lord,' says Magrieta, 'perhaps I should have. Has his office always been quite so empty?'

'Yes, but now there is *nothing*.' Isabel looks around. 'Not a plant or a stone or a picture or a photo, not a single blade of grass. Just the computer and the few books on the shelf.'

She looks around some more, moves some books aside, opens and shuts the desk drawers. 'Not even a calendar,' she says. She reads the titles of the few books on the shelf aloud: '*The New Penguin History of the World*, *The War that Ended Peace*, *An Intimate History of Humanity*, *The Moral Animal*, *The Devils* by Dostoevsky. *Moral Tribes*. Impressive. What do you deduce about Potsdam from these titles?'

'I really don't know, Isabel,' says Magrieta. 'Were there always so few books here?'

'I think so,' says the girl, 'perhaps they just look fewer today because he's not here. Have you ever heard him listen to music?'

'No,' says Magrieta. 'I have no idea what he would listen to.'

'Bach,' says Isabel.

'How can you be so sure?' asks Magrieta, even more perturbed.

'I'm just guessing. Bach, now and again a bit of jazz for variety. Miles Davis maybe. Coltrane.'

'Lord, Isabel,' Magrieta exclaims, 'how on earth do you know all these things?!'

'I'm telling you, I'm just guessing.' Isabel goes down on her haunches and inspects every desk drawer again. 'Nothing here,' she says. 'Not even a thumb tack or a paper clip. Nothing. If there had been anything, it's gone now too. I should have cased his drawers earlier. I should have hacked his computer,' she repeats. 'You shouldn't have stopped me. Now it's too late. Fucking fuck a fucking buck.'

'I can't *believe* it,' says Magrieta, 'I've been working with this man for more than a year, and I still don't have the vaguest idea about his personal life. I don't know if he has a partner, I don't know what music he listens to – nothing, I know *nothing* about him!'

'Personally I think he's walked into the sea,' says Isabel.

'What makes you think that?!' Magrieta exclaims. This is not something she wants to hear now.

'I just have a sudden sense,' says Isabel.

'Since when have you had this sense?'

'Since just now. I've just had it.'

'What do you know that you're not telling me?' Magrieta asks suspiciously.

'Nothing,' says Isabel.

'But on what are you basing this sense?'

'On my gut feeling.'

'Do you trust it?'

'Yes, I trust it.'

'Your sense is that he walked into the sea, not that he did himself in in some other way?'

'No, my sense is the sea.'

'How often do you have this kind of sense?'

'Oh, now and again,' says Isabel blithely.

'And you trust it?' Magrieta asks again.

'Yes, sometimes, not always.'

'Do you trust it *now*?'

'Yes, sort of.'

'And you don't find it disturbing to have such a sense?'

'No, why would I? It's just a sense, a hunch, I don't know it for *certain*.'

'I must go and look for him,' says Magrieta.

Isabel laughs. 'How are you going to do *that*?'

'I don't know,' says Magrieta. 'I'll have to think of a way. But I'm really panicking now!'

'Don't panic,' says the girl. 'Go and sit down. It's no use hanging around here in his office. I'll make you a cup of tea. I'll phone the Bureau's headquarters. They must have an address for him.'

'I'm going to look for this man,' says Magrieta, suddenly vehement. 'You're right. This is no time to panic. Even if I have to dredge him up from the bottom of the sea and make him sit down at his computer again. Don't *laugh*.'

'I'm not laughing,' says the girl, but her face is flushed with suppressing her laughter. 'And if he doesn't *want* to be found?'

'Isabel,' says Magrieta, 'what do you know that you're not telling me?'

'Nothing, I know *nothing*,' she says, but Magrieta can see that she's ready to bust a gut laughing.

*

Because they both come home from work relatively late, Magrieta and Willem go for their walk in the vineyard just before six. They don't take the same route as the one on which she met the woman in the tent. A low mist cloud drifts in front of the mountain. The colours are saturated – rich greens, deep blues. Willem tells her about his day. Magrieta dawdles behind. She is preoccupied. She hears only a snatch here and there of what he's saying.

He grills fish for them. She makes vegetables. He kisses her neck, touches her buttocks while she's preparing the vegetables. She is still preoccupied. She tells him that Markus Potsdam is gone. What does she mean, gone? It doesn't look as if he's planning to come back soon, she says. On what grounds does she say that? His office has been completely emptied – not that there was much to empty – and he didn't say where he was going or how long he was planning to be away. He trusts that she and Isabel will take over the reins. He left them a list of assignments. But that's so irresponsible, Willem exclaims – he can surely not expect it of her, that's no way for a director to behave! That's true, she has to admit. But Potsdam could be back in a week or two – his secretiveness is nothing new, that's how he does things, she says. (Also to comfort herself.)

There's also no point in telling Willem that Isabel has a feeling – a hunch, a suspicion – that Potsdam walked into the sea. He would simply dismiss the idea as ludicrous.

Willem is impatient. He wants to make love to her. But she doesn't want to be made love to tonight. She is upset, she is preoccupied. She wants to sit on the stoep and think. The woman in the vineyard succeeded in disappearing from her own life. It looks as if Potsdam had something similar in mind and may have succeeded in it. Maybe he did, maybe he didn't.

The bedroom is companionably warm. Willem caresses her body appreciatively. She lets him be. At first penetration feels unwelcome, but then she is borne along in spite of herself. But during the orgasm it's Potsdam whom, for a moment, she suddenly conjures up vividly in her mind.

*

The next day she looks closely at the list of instructions on her computer. Nicely, neatly, chronologically, Potsdam has set out for her what her duties are and who she should see in the following weeks: which agents (as he still refers to the associates), which donors, plus the next trip she must take to the Eastern Cape. She shows this to Isabel. So he's planning to be absent for at least the next seven or eight weeks, says Magrieta.

'Fuck a buck,' the girl says.

'I have two options,' says Magrieta. 'The one is I meekly take over the reins. See all the agents I'm supposed to see. Every single one plus the donors. Carry on as if nothing's changed. The other option is I drop everything and try to find out where Potsdam is and whether he's okay.'

Isabel looks at her askance. 'Since when do you feel so responsible for the man? Are you in love with him or what?'

'No,' says Magrieta, 'no, Lord, no! I'm not in love with him. I just feel responsible for him. I feel I neglected my duty towards him.'

'What duty?!'

'I could see there was something amiss. I could have asked him what the matter was, whether he was okay.'

'Is Potsdam the kind of man you can ask something like that?'

'I don't know. I suppose not. But still. Do you still think he walked into the sea?'

'It's just a hunch,' says Isabel. 'Hunches aren't always reliable.'

'Your hunch isn't perhaps telling you *where* he walked into the sea?'

Isabel laughs and against her will Magrieta has to laugh along. 'Relax,' says Isabel. 'I'll help you. I phoned. The Bureau has only his Bureau address. I informed them that he's missing. But we'll find out something. *Someone* has to know.'

So that's what she has to show for it, says Magrieta. She should never have taken this crap job, she says. She should have looked for something in her own field from the outset. Perhaps even have crawled back on her knees to her former department head. He would have liked *that*. She should have got away from here while she still could. Then she wouldn't be stuck here worrying about Potsdam's welfare, with a job she doesn't want to do. Lord! Could Potsdam not like any normal person have given them notice that he wanted to go away for a while?

'Like any normal person give notice that he's planning to walk into the sea,' Isabel says.

'Don't rub it in and don't mock,' says Magrieta. 'I'm upset.'

'Who knows,' says the girl, 'he may be back sooner than we think. You know what an oddball he is. There could be a thousand and one reasons why he suddenly decided he had to be off.'

'Suddenly had to walk into the sea,' says Magrieta bitterly.

'It's just a hunch,' says Isabel. 'I should never even have said it. I'm sure he's okay.'

'You're just saying that to make me feel better.'

'Maybe, but even so. Relax. You may be blowing this thing up out of proportion. I'm *sure* the man is okay.'

'At the bottom of the sea, yes. Don't laugh.'

'I'm not laughing,' says the girl.

'Sure, you can laugh,' says Magrieta. 'You're young, you're pretty, you have a future. I got myself into this mess through my own foolish actions. And now I'm stuck with these bloody complications as well. And don't *you* also abandon the sinking ship and leave me here on my own with the mess. When do you hear about your scholarship?'

'Soon. But don't worry. I'm not planning to abandon you to your misery.'

Magrieta sends an SMS to Markus Potsdam: *Markus, are you okay? Please let us know. We are worried.* No reply. Deafening silence. Perhaps threw his phone into a river or the sea like the woman in the vineyard.

*

She goes to see Deneys Swiegers. Perhaps he knows something about Potsdam. Perhaps he has an address or something – after all, Swiegers has been involved with the Bureau for some time. She tells him what happened. Swiegers is shocked, he finds it quite outrageous of Potsdam to disappear like that without informing them in advance, or letting them know where he is or how long he will be away.

But no, he has no information regarding Potsdam, he doesn't know anything about his personal life either. They've always had only the most essential contact regarding Bureau matters. But he recalls that his assistant, Bertie Oberholzer, once mentioned that he and Potsdam sometimes played chess. Perhaps he knows something about him.

So when Oberholzer soon thereafter puts his spiteful head around the door, Swiegers calls him in. Mistrustfully he enters the room. Swiegers introduces Magrieta to him.

She believes he knows Markus Potsdam, she says.

Yes? he says warily.

She explains the situation briefly, without incriminating Potsdam too much, in case he and this distrustful fellow are bosom friends (highly unlikely, but you never know) and he refuses to say anything more.

She believes they played chess together, she says. Does he perhaps have any idea where Potsdam lives, where she could perhaps get hold of him?

They only played chess, says Oberholzer, they didn't have personal conversations.

'Was Potsdam already working for the Bureau for Continuing Education at that time?' she tries again.

But Bertie Oberholzer is as headstrong as a child resisting his parents' request to recite a poem. It's clear that he mistrusts the situation. He doesn't know, he says, as he's said, they only played chess together, they didn't really have friendly relations.

'Anything you may know about Markus Potsdam that could shed light on where he is at the moment?' she asks feebly, the wind taken out of her sails by the man's curt reaction.

'I think Potsdam has a house in Kogelberg,' he says. 'Or at least he had it a while ago. He sometimes went there for weekends. My sister knows somebody who lives there who told her.'

Magrieta exclaims gratefully. She thanks him extravagantly. On his way out Oberholzer turns around and concedes: 'A blue house.'

When he's left, Deneys Swiegers says: 'He's struggling to complete his doctorate. Very easily distracted.'

*

She has a possible address for Potsdam, at least, she tells Willem that evening. Apparently he has a house in Kogelberg. And you're considering going to look for the guy there? Willem asks. Where would you start – go from door to door? Apparently it's a blue house, she says.

Don't be silly, Magrieta, says Willem, let the guy go. Why would you want to go and look for him? If you want to resign, go ahead and resign. It's not your responsibility to arrange for someone to take his place. Not after this highly unprofessional conduct on his part. That's simply not how one runs an organisation.

Magrieta says nothing. She sits brooding in silence in the sitting room. She doesn't want to join him for a walk in the vineyard. You're being silly, Magrieta, says Willem, you're being unnecessarily stubborn. For a reasonable woman you can sometimes be very unreasonable.

(They must both be thinking of her period of unbridled unreasonableness, when her reckless conduct made nothing of driving their relationship to the brink of destruction.)

*

The next morning Isabel announces that there is someone to see Magrieta. To her surprise it's Bertie Oberholzer. He's standing in front of her door sheepishly. She invites him in. She thinks, he's bringing more information regarding Markus Potsdam. Sit down, she invites him. He looks less unfriendly today, but crestfallen. He's still wearing shorts and boots, and only a red checked skirt, apparently unaware of the cold.

He sits down. He clearly has something to impart. He waits. Deneys Swiegers' duck is a failure, he says. He's using outdated technology. He's embarked on an experiment that costs time and money, and it's going to lead nowhere.

Magrieta thinks: What have we here?!

'But he's pigheaded. He won't listen to anybody. Especially not to me.'

Bertie stops talking. It looks as if he has more to unload. It looks as if he has suddenly been overtaken by a great emotion that he can control only with an effort.

'I helped do the programming,' he says, 'for that useless duck. Not that he'll give me credit for it. Oh no, not Swiegers!'

He gazes in front of him, tears well up in his eyes.

'Sometimes I think Swiegers despises me,' he says, 'it's as simple as that. He despises me.'

'How can you think that?' she exclaims, surprised.

'He despises me,' he repeats, 'that is simply that, once and for all.' He struggles to control his tears. 'Swiegers is selfish. He thinks the duck belongs to him alone. He's totally infatuated with that useless thing! You would swear . . .' But further than that he does not get, because he has to fight the tears, he sniffs, he tries every so often to wipe his nose with the back of his hand. Isabel peeks around the door, she must have heard there was something going on here. Her face is red. Magrieta signals to her it's okay, everything is under control.

'Bertie,' she says, 'calm down. Sit up straight. Sit up straight and blow your nose. I'm sure it's not that bad.' She pushes a box of tissues across her desk to him.

Bertie looks up and says, with a small, bitter smile: 'You have no idea how bad it is.'

No, Magrieta thinks, I don't. No point in asking him about Potsdam now. She has no taste for this – to act as a shoulder for this man to cry on about how Swiegers treats him. In any case, she can't imagine that Swiegers really *despises* him – he has complained about Bertie on occasion, but that's far from despising him. He doesn't look like the kind of man who goes around despising people left, right and centre. She has only ever found him balanced and rational. Bertie Oberholzer is probably imagining all sorts of things. His ruddy complexion alone is enough to tell you that he's a fellow who easily gets worked up. And why he should elect *her* for his unbosoming and emotional discharge baffles her. She's not unfriendly, but she doesn't exactly radiate tremendous warmth to strangers.

With an effort she manages to console him after a fashion and get him out of her office.

In the meantime she's fed up and put out, because she has to travel to the Eastern Cape again. It's the first of Potsdam's neatly laid-out assignments she must execute. There are two new associates (agents) with whom she has to consult. She has to get in touch with Agent Green again. She must see whether Nonki Jansen van Rensburg is making headway with the township project and whether she's not finding it too demanding. Does she feel like it? No. What she really wants to do now, at this moment, is to get into her car and drive to Kogelberg, to go and ferret the damned Potsdam out of his blue house. Or at least pick up his scent and follow him from there. Even if it is to the bottom of the sea. The way she's feeling at the moment, she'll haul him out of there half-drowned, because in the last few days she's been angry and worried by turns, and today she's angry – she really doesn't need the complication of his disappearance in her life.

*

When Bertie Oberholzer has left, Magrieta and Isabel have lunch at the restaurant on the second floor, just under the Bureau on the third floor. In the distance Stellenboschberg is visible from here – somewhat obscured by the buildings in the foreground. All the buildings in this complex are a uniform steel grey. The rental for the Bureau offices must be very high. What was Potsdam *thinking*, or did he have no say in the matter, Magrieta wonders.

It's the end of July. It's cold. Snow is expected on the mountains. Isabel is wearing fingerless gloves and a beanie. On her otherwise pale cheeks there are two red spots of cold.

She says: 'Tell me the story of the duck. I was listening at the door, but I couldn't hear it all.'

Magrieta says: 'You're going to laugh.'

Isabel says: 'I know.'

'The man has a problem with Swiegers' robo-duck, he thinks it's a failure, and he thinks Swiegers despises him. But that said, I'm going to the Eastern Cape again next week. I have to go and minister to the needs of a lot of agents again.'

'You're not going to tell head office they can stuff their Bureau up their arse?'

'No,' says Magrieta, 'I'm too fucking decent. And I need time to look for something else, even though I feel like going to look for Potsdam today already.'

'Like a dog dragging a rabbit out of its lair.'

'Yes,' says Magrieta, 'something like that.' (She remembers her father telling her that a dog can't easily get at a pangolin, because it rolls itself into a ball when threatened. Perhaps Potsdam is making himself inaccessible in similar fashion.)

Eleven

Early August. Huge clouds come rolling over the mountain in the morning. Icy conditions are forecast for the Western Cape. Dead quiet in the mornings – no human, no animal or bird stirs in the early morning. Everybody who does not have a proper roof over their heads is frozen in winter sleep brought on by drink or drug. Or curled up in lairs. This is not the time for the homeless to wander around at night. Who knows if the woman in the vineyard could get away in time, and if the victors (rapists and worse) are sleeping cosily snuggled up in the plundered tent?

She resolves to close the door of the Bureau behind her as soon as she's made her way through Potsdam's neatly typed list. Whether Potsdam has returned by then or not.

Her usual shuttle service comes to collect her from her home very early in the morning. The driver, Greg, smells of smoke. Normally they talk, but it's too early in the morning for that and, besides, the smell of smoke makes her nauseous. She's sure he's Afrikaans-speaking but they always speak English to each other. She sits in the back of the car and gazes at the early-morning landscape flashing by. Small wind wavelets on a watery surface.

On the N2, near the airport off-ramp, they have to slow down and then stop, for what was presumably a recent service-delivery protest. Piles of scattered refuse are still littering the road, as are rocks, two smouldering car tyres, branches and logs. The protest must have taken place earlier that morning or the previous night, because there are still people standing around – mainly women and children, some with folded arms, others in little huddles. (Why aren't the children at school?) In the background a few men are loitering, hands in pockets, heads drawn into necks against the cold. It doesn't look as if anybody is planning anything more. But impossible to know if the protest action will flare up again. On the other side of the road is a lone police car. There is not enough stuff in the road to block it – just enough to slow the traffic, because the cars in both directions must take turns to drive cautiously through the rocks and rubble and smouldering tyres. Magrieta is impatient, she has a plane to catch. She does not want to stare too openly, scared to make eye contact with someone. She tries to make herself as invisible as possible in the back of the car. (Concealed privilege.) A short distance ahead of her she sees a young girl rolling a tyre away from the road and, suddenly, from the corner of her eye, a child picking up a stone – almost in slow motion – but while he's stooping down, a woman with dreadlocks gets hold of the back of his shirt to restrain him. An eerie, soundless, half-static tableau. It takes a while before they can drive on, there are still quite a few cars ahead of them. Greg passes an annoyed comment, she doesn't know if it's directed at her. She doesn't feel like sounding him out for his true feelings. She does ask him if he often comes across this kind of protest. He shrugs indifferently. Not too often. At last it's their turn to go. She is *just* in time for her flight.

Arriving at the airport in PE, this time she rents a car. She does not avail herself again of the services of the guy with the two tame squirrels (Poppy and Poopy) and his girlfriend with the scar. (Grey-blue coat.) She wanted to stay at the guesthouse with the worried young woman again, but they were fully booked.

Arriving at the new guesthouse, she's told that she's been moved to yet another place, further down in the town (behind the cathedral, near where the man in the wheelchair almost ran over her and other bystanders). No reasons are tendered for the move. The new guesthouse strikes her as suspect. The small entrance hall is hardly partitioned off from the dining room. On the right are a number of round tables with red plastic tablecloths. On the left is a wall with a large mirror and an alcove with a wooden surface on which there is a lone plastic container with Post Toasties. Seated at one of the tables is a woman with heavy make-up. The hair on the side of her head has been shaved, and the remaining upright quiff is in shades of black, yellow and peroxide – white as a tuft of wintry grass. At another table a woman with a synthetic, amber-coloured mop of curly hair is attending to her cellphone.

The woman on duty takes Magrieta to her room. The passage is long. Magrieta's room is the second on the left. The room is small, dark and ice cold. The space is almost wholly occupied by a double bed, covered with a thin synthetic duvet. A single wardrobe in dark wood in the corner. The room smells of insecticide and mothballs. The place is a brothel, she thinks. She doesn't mind staying in a brothel. The ways and means of prostitutes interest her. But the stifling smell of mothballs is already irritating her nose and that means she won't get any sleep. She checks out summarily.

She needs to find another place to stay in a hurry. Isabel must arrange it for her. She lets Magrieta know that she can choose between a fancy B&B and a single room in a student hostel – it's still university vacation, later than usual this year. Because she's not sure of the state of the Bureau's finances, Magrieta chooses the single room. A narrow cot, desk in front of the window, hand basin in one corner, built-in wooden wardrobe, heater high up on the wall above the bed; the bathroom down the passage. Magrieta likes the room, it's like a convent cell. It suits her mood. She remembers the disquieting tableau of the little protest action on the way to the airport. At the back of her mind still the resolve – probably ridiculous – to go and look for Potsdam. As soon as she's done here. May he be regretting his decision already and be waiting for her at the office on her return. Although with each passing day that she doesn't hear from him, she thinks it less likely. She misses his running SMS commentaries. On the spur of the moment she sends him an SMS: *I am in the Eastern Cape; I'm working my way through your list. Let me know how you are.*

No reply. The first thing he did was probably to get rid of his cellphone (like the woman in the vineyard).

When she wants to take her antidepressant, she can't find the pills in her toiletry bag. She must have left them at home. She was running late when Greg came to pick her up. Three days without that useless pill will probably not make that much of a difference, she thinks.

She meets Nonki Jansen van Rensburg again in the same coffee shop. Her hair has been cut short and dyed black. She's wearing Doc Martens and a long black coat. She is pale. She looks older. This time she's wearing black fingerless gloves. She holds her cup in both hands. Her fingers are red. She's resigned, she says, she can no longer carry on with her project in the township. The situation there is too much for her. Nobody in the white town realises the conditions under which these people have to live. She can't handle it any more, the way the animals suffer there. And to top it all her handbag with her tablet and cellphone in it was stolen while she was putting up posters. Some of the group working with her know who did it, but they don't want to tell her.

And the poet with the dreadlocks, is he still here? asks Magrieta. (Her instruction from Potsdam the previous time had been to make sure that Nonki didn't fraternise too much with the natives. Count on Potsdam to make such a politically incorrect statement.) He's gone back to Gauteng, says Nonki, his residency with the department is over. She assumes the woman from Iceland is also long gone, Magrieta says. Yes, she too, says Nonki.

In a second-hand bookstore Magrieta buys, for a song, copies of *Waiting for Godot* and *Gold and Workers 1886–1924* by Luli Callinicos. Also a small – avowedly essential – guide to human evolution. The day is cold, but clear. No howling wind and pouring rain as on her previous visit. No worm flying in the night.

That afternoon she has an appointment with an archaeologist at the natural history museum. Magrieta likes natural history museums. It's the single bright spot of this visit. Agent Buitendach (Doctor Ben

Buitendach), the man she has to meet, is short, his eyes small and as brown as two paw-paw pips. His black hair is shoulder-length and unwashed. The big room to which he takes her smells overpoweringly of bones. (Isabel would not last long here. The bones would give her the creeps; the smell would probably make her puke.) He introduces her to his colleague, Barry Cilliers, a palaeontologist – a man with attentive eyes and a fuzzy outline. She's read that Buitendach has excavated the body of a two-thousand-year-old Bushman. She'd like to see it. For reasons of political correctness, and so as not to offend people, it's no longer on display, he says.

They take her to a smaller back room. Behind a black plastic curtain, covered in a sheet of black plastic, lies the body. The little Bushman is lying on his side, his legs drawn up high, his arms between his legs. Hard to believe it's the body of an adult. A shapely round head, broad cheekbones, so characteristic of the San people. Tiny ears. Tufts of hair still visible in places, also the beads around the neck. The feet are small and delicate, a child's feet. Because of the leaves the body was swaddled in and the dry heat of the environment in which he was buried, his body has remained preserved for two thousand years. Buitendach explains that the toxin from the poison bulb plant (*Boophone disticha*) prevented insects from laying their eggs in the body. The leaves are still visible in places – very thin, and so similar in colour to the skin that it's difficult to tell skin and leaf apart. As if the skin itself is thin as flaky pastry. Thin as thin sheets of rolled-out Plasticine.

It is possible, explains Buitendach, that the body was swaddled in poison bulb leaves not only to preserve it, but to help the dead person to enter the other world in a trance state.

'The other world is leaky as a boat, says Quignard,' his colleague says quietly.

Magrieta darts him a quick glance, not sure that she's heard him correctly.

Buitendach tells her that the poison bulb was found in some other hollows in the ground, lined with grass. Some archaeologists believe that the Bushmen stored the plant in this way, others think the holes were spaces granting access to another world, because the poison bulb plant induces hallucinations when ingested.

Afterwards they have tea in the cafeteria of the museum.

Magrieta is intrigued by Barry Cilliers' pronouncement. Who is Quignard? What did he mean? Cilliers is shy. He drinks his tea in delicate sips. Keeps his gaze averted. His answer is evasive: Quignard is a contemporary French writer, he translates from Latin, Chinese and Greek. Magrieta thinks, what does that have to do with anything, what he translates from? Why is the man so evasive? She wants to know about the other world that leaks like a boat. She wants to know what it's supposed to mean. She tries to draw Cilliers out. Does Quignard see death as the other world, she asks, or does he see the other world as parallel to ours? Cilliers shrugs, he's not sure. That's all, nothing further, just he's not sure. This irritates her: so why did he even *mention* it?

Perhaps the woman in the vineyard had hoped her tent, like the hollows in the ground, would grant access to another reality. She could tell them about the woman in the vineyard, but she's suddenly impatient with both of them. Buitendach's attention is elsewhere; Cilliers' outline is too fuzzy, he's too evasive. Why would he be so cagey as not to want to elaborate on Quignard's statement?

When she takes her leave, she tells Buitendach that she wants to drop in at the Department of Ichthyology to see the coelacanth, she didn't get round to it last time. Fish aren't exactly her thing, she says, but she does like whales a lot.

She hurries to the ichthyology department before it closes. The coelacanth is almost five feet long and pale yellow. The skin on one side has been removed so that the internal organs are visible. A lobe-finned fish, but not from the group of lobe-finned fish from which the tetrapods developed. In humans and other tetrapods the lobe fins have adapted to form arms, legs, wings. Before the enthralling discovery of this first living coelacanth it was assumed that it became extinct before the dinosaurs, in the Cretaceous period, because the coelacanths (Coelacanthiformes) were the first branching from the extinct line of lobe-finned fish, when plants started colonising the dry land and coral reefs started expanding in the sea, 425 million years ago.

In its natural state the coelacanth is a beautiful, purplish-blue fish, with iridescent markings, but this one is a dead, botched specimen. Today she finds it ugly, even a bit repulsive.

In the late afternoon she has a bowl of soup in a restaurant, drinks a glass of wine and returns to her convent cell in the early evening. She reads in Beckett that Vladimir and Estragon tell each other that the dead talk about their lives. To have lived is not enough for them, they have to talk about it. To have been dead is not enough for them, they say. She looks at the illustrations in Luli Callinicos' book (the first in the series *A People's History of South Africa*). She knows so much about the history of the earth, she thinks, so much about the evolution of the invertebrates, and so little of the history of the people who went down in the mines.

Once again on the spur of the moment, in an attempt to catch Potsdam unawares, to provoke him, she sends him an SMS late that night: *Did you know that the other world is leaky as a boat?*

*

The next morning she wakes up in a bad mood. Strange incidents from her youth had returned to her in the early morning. She has an unpleasant taste in her mouth. Her coccyx feels numb. She feels angry and weepy at the same time. She misses her child. She holds it against her daughter that she so seldom sends word of herself.

All day long she feels disgruntled and out of sorts. She doesn't want to be here and she doesn't want to be at home either. Especially not at the Bureau, however much she likes Isabel. And *she* will also leave one of these days. (Just like her daughter, to start a new life in another country. *She* stays behind, sometimes overwhelmed with longing for the child.) The second person (agent) she was supposed to meet today sends word that he can't make it any longer. That her time is being wasted like this unsettles her even more.

Who does she find in the coffee shop where she has to meet Agent Green that afternoon? None other than Agent Oliver in his wheelchair, in exactly the same spot as a year ago. Like then, he's sitting with a pot of tea, a slice of carrot cake with sprinkles, and his Kindle. Her hackles rise immediately. As she walks past him to the only open table in the back of the coffee shop, she doesn't greet him, but murmurs softly, fucking fascist. Softly, but loudly enough for him to hear.

'What's that you said, Miss?' he asks.

Magrieta suddenly feels something akin to Kundalini energy shooting up her spine. 'I said fucking fascist,' she says.

The man swings his wheelchair around at her furiously. 'Can you repeat that?' he asks.

'Yes,' she says. 'Fucking fascist.'

By this time the attention of all the patrons is fixed on them. The man beckons to the waitress. His face is blood red. Somebody gets hold of Magrieta's arm. It's Agent Green. She hadn't even seen him come in. 'You won't get away with this!' Agent Oliver shouts after her, seething, but Green is already steering Magrieta out of the coffee shop with a firm grip on her arm, to another place across the street.

Magrieta is trembling. Her knees feel numb.

'What was *that* all about?' Agent Green asks.

'I don't know,' she says. 'It's probably because I left my stupid pills at home.'

They order something to drink. Magrieta's heart is still beating wildly. She asks Green if he knows anything about Potsdam's personal life. (Grasping, with beating heart, at straws.) No, says Green, they only connected about Bureau matters. Agent Green starts talking nineteen to the dozen. He's probably trying to distract her from the ugly scene of earlier. But she can't focus on what he's saying. He talks and he gesticulates – with his tiny mouth and his round cheeks and his fleshy palms and finger joints, and his fingers spaced wide on the palm and bending far backwards like the illustrated hands in the book about Japanese tantras.

He tells her that at school he was an outsider because he wasn't good at sport. Then he started reading Marx in matric and that distinguished him from the other children. At university he was a hardline Marxist but now his great interest is Bizarro fiction. Does she remember the evening when the writer from Iceland came to talk to them about it? Yes, says Magrieta, she remembers. (That was the last time she spoke to Professor Mogoerane – the first and the last time. In that room, thick with smoke, he put his great, generous mouth to her ear and told her about the Soutpansberg project. Which has probably ground to a halt now that Mogoerane has left the country.) The more bizarre the better, says Agent Green. The more bizarre, the rarer, the more it deviates from the mainstream, the greater the satisfaction, the greater the pleasure it gives him. He is attracted to apocalyptic scenarios. Fiction dealing with the body as landscape interests him. *Warrior Wolf Women of the Wasteland. Squid Pulp Blues. The Deadheart Shelters. The Menstruating Mall.* Kmart realism also interests him. But he's not all that taken with the New Sincerity. He prefers the neutral voice to the painfully sincere voice. Frankness about personal loss he finds repulsive.

Why is he telling her all these things, Magrieta wonders. Fuck Potsdam for leaving them in the lurch like that. She's not going to let him get away with it, whatever story he comes up with, and he'd better have a good excuse. If he comes back at all, of course – and that's by no means a foregone conclusion. Wouldn't it be hilarious if he's taken off for good, she thinks bitterly.

'Stripped sentences,' says Agent Green, 'underemphasised dialogue—'

Magrieta gets to her feet abruptly, interrupts Green. 'I'm sorry,' she says, 'I have to go. A friend of mine finds Bizarro fiction uninteresting, nothing more than a diluted form of surrealism. Goodbye.' (She asked Jakob Wolmarans about it in Jameson Bay.)

She walks back quickly to her room. A beggar puts out his hand and she flings him a disapproving comment. Her cheeks are still burning. With shame? The scene she made was surely unnecessary. In her convent cell she sits down on the bed. What now?

She reads the opening chapters in Luli Callinicos. South Africa before Industrial Times. The Gold Rush. Deep-level Mining. The Randlords. Should she let Potsdam know how resentful she feels towards him today? But what would be the point of tormenting him further with her messages if he's already feeling tormented? At seven o'clock she walks down to the town again, past the natural history museum where the Bushman is lying, past the administration building, past the Department of Ichthyology where the yellow-pale fish hangs, motionless. She eats another bowl of soup and drinks three glasses of wine that leave her unpleasantly befuddled. It's cold when she walks back, she folds her coat closer over her body. The campus is deserted. In a big lawned square poinsettias are blooming. In the entrance foyer of the hostel a pretty, young, dark-skinned student with dreadlocks is sitting reading at a little heater. Magrieta has not come across anybody else in her corridor. In her convent cell she immediately switches on the wall heater.

She reads another few chapters of *Gold and Workers*. She pages through the evolution guide. She looks at the depictions of reconstructions of Lucy (*Australopithecus afarensis*), of the head of a female *Homo floresiensis*, and of a Neanderthal child. All the reconstructions remarkably lifelike. The eyes in particular already show signs of something human. A consciousness other than that of the great apes. Between seven and five million years ago the line of the anthropoid ape split from the lines of the chimpanzees and bonobos, our closest relatives. About five million years for *Homo sapiens* to evolve, an animal with a complex brain and consciousness, and what is his destination? Death. More than five million years for an animal to evolve with a painful awareness of his own mortality. Evolution is indifferent to results and consequences.

She receives three WhatsApp photos from her daughter. Magrieta is pleasantly surprised! They were apparently taken in a natural history museum. In one of the photos it looks as if the girl is standing before a cabinet with skulls – difficult to tell exactly, because her face is brightly lit, but the background is dark. In another she's standing in silhouette in front of something that looks like part of a whale skeleton – only the shoulder blade and flipper visible. And a photo of an entire whale skeleton, from behind, taken from the tail end.

Thought you'd like this, her daughter writes. Smiling in all the photos. The child is okay. Free of the mother's fretful interference, according to the woman in the vineyard. Of course she likes the photo of the whale, her child knows her well enough! Of course the sheer size of the animal amazes her, the mighty skull with baleen like a curtain, like a waterfall; the overwhelming orchestration of the ribs and tail vertebrae! Of course Magrieta is glad that her daughter thinks of her in foreign countries. It's not easy for her that the child is far away, but she never wants to burden her with her longing.

She packs her case. Before going to sleep, she quickly googles Quignard. He does indeed translate from Latin, Chinese and Greek, and he has a penetrating gaze. But nowhere is his pronouncement on the other world mentioned.

*

Back in Stellenbosch in the days that follow she's brusque and impatient with Willem. She makes quite a few scathing and sneering comments at him, and when one evening she strikes at him again like a poisonous snake, Willem says, that's enough, she can't take it out on him every time her head's out of kilter or she's on the wrong pill or whatever. Just say the word and he'll pack his bags tonight and be off. He loves her, a lot, but he can't bear the brunt every time she takes a dip.

Magrieta gets a fright. Instantly, she suffers intense remorse. She remembers all of a sudden how she would tell her father she was sorry before he gave her and her brother a hiding. Please, she'll never do it again, she promised (while her brother kept quiet, white as a sheet). It was never much use, because her father gave them a hiding all the same. She cried and performed, which convinced her father that she'd been chastised enough. Once her mother sat down on the belt to prevent her father from hitting them. It was terrible. It was almost worse than a hiding.

With tremor and trepidation she seduces Willem that evening. She sits on top of him, like Kali implanted on top of Shiva, in his incarnation as a corpse. With each rhythmic thrust she drives Willem closer to surrender, until at long last he falls back vanquished with a cry from the depth of his throat.

Twelve

A few days later Willem has to rush to his ailing mother in Pretoria, whose condition has suddenly deteriorated overnight. In the same week Isabel has to go to Johannesburg for a follow-up interview in connection with her scholarship application.

Magrieta does what she must. She eats with the donors. She barely makes the effort any more to be friendly, let alone flirtatious. If they want to give money, that's just fine. If they don't want to give, that's also just fine. It's not her problem. It's Potsdam's, wherever he may be. (She has no idea what that man is capable of doing or not doing.) She meets the agents in the town and in Cape Town. She is succinct, she is efficient. She arranges what has to be arranged. She administers the associates' incoming reports, she finds out from the finance department whether there are still sufficient funds for her and Isabel's salaries. (There are, to her surprise. What did she expect: that Potsdam absconded with all the available funds?! Started a small business with it? Marched into the sea with the last of it, in crackling-fresh two-hundred-rand notes?)

In the late afternoon Magrieta walks the dog in the vineyard. She doesn't walk far, because she's not in the mood for walking. She pays no attention to the lovely mountains and the shifting cloud patterns. She doesn't look for signs of habitation (a mud-covered garment, a shoe, a charred chicken bone). She doesn't prick up her ears for sounds, for traces of the secret argot blowing on the wind (*come here poes, fuck off poes*). She just keeps her eye fixed on the path in front of her. She doesn't see the spotted eagle owl sitting on one of the vineyard posts and later flying off soundlessly.

The evening is long and the house is quiet. She doesn't normally notice how quiet it is. (The silence sounds to her like the soundless susurration of the indifferent and expanding universe.) She's usually too distracted, too busy running after agents, postponing her own life.

The dog follows her everywhere in the house. The dog is making an appeal to her. She wants something from her, but Magrieta doesn't know what it is. It's Willem's dog, she probably gets something from him she doesn't get from her. Click-click-click go her nails when she follows Magrieta through the house. The soft click-click-click is the only noise breaking the silence.

She can almost not bear this silence at home in the evenings. It's no use switching on the radio. But she doesn't want to listen to music either, especially not to her favourite music. She has an odd sense that it will violate the silence. That the silence is something she must endure. Nothing dispels it. It presses against her eardrums, it presses against her chest.

She's glad when Jakob phones and asks if he can come and have tea with her. She hasn't seen him for a long time. She's too busy at the Bureau; she doesn't see anybody any more. She makes a big pot of tea. He drinks one cup of tea after the other. He is excited. His novel is coming along. While talking, he strokes the dog's fur distractedly. The main character is an archaeologist. He's working on a site in the desert. He's part of a team, but he keeps to himself. They dig up a statue. Its eyes have inlays of shell and obsidian. Shell for the white of the eye. Obsidian for the irises.

Where is the desert? she asks.

It's an imaginary desert, he says.

She has to think of Mosul, she says, where Jonah's tomb was destroyed. Does he remember, they talked about it in Jameson Bay, after she'd seen the beached fish.

He remembers.

Is Mosul in the desert? she asks.

He's not sure, he says, but *his* desert is an imaginary desert.

The last time she was in Albany West, she says, she saw, in the natural history museum, the body of a two-thousand-year-old Bushman. It was excavated in a cave in the Langkloof, near Joubertina.

Oh yes? he says, interested.

It was swaddled in the leaves of the poison bulb plant *Boophone disticha*, which prevented insects from laying their eggs in the corpse, but also perhaps to help the dead person to reach the other world, because it can induce hallucinations when ingested. One of the guys there quoted Quignard: The other world is leaky as a boat. She's wondered a lot about the meaning of it, she says. What does he think?

It's a multivalent statement, says Jakob, it can be read in so many ways, he'll have to think about it.

Magrieta says for her the other world or underworld is the Hadean era, the beginning, the early gestation period of the earth, when there was nothing, when circumstances were hostile to all life. She would like to witness the origin and diversification of life in the geological eras unfolding before her eyes. The inception of the first unicellular and later multicellular organisms from the bubbling primal soup. The inexorable proliferation and diversification of life forms in the Cambrian period – the algae, the mosses, the sponges, the jellyfish, corals, sea anemones, the flatworms – without anus or with multiple anuses.

Jakob says, yes, it's a pity it couldn't all have been documented. The unfolding of the first fern, for instance.

In the Upper Silurian, she says, and the moment – moment! – in the Devonian period when the lobe-finned fish cautiously set the first half-formed limb on solid ground.

When were the giant dragonflies?

In the Carboniferous period, she says, when the sea began contracting and left space for swamps.

And when was the snowball earth? he asks, *that* he can hardly conceive.

Yes, she says, inconceivable, the earth covered in a thick layer of ice for millennia.

Imagine, he says, how it speeds through space ice cold and dead quiet.

Yes, says Magrieta, in anticipation of the great explosion of germination and multiplication of the Cambrian.

He's read somewhere that silence is necessary for the maturing of ideas. Then the snowball earth is like an idea growing into maturity – God's idea of maturation.

God has strange ideas, says Magrieta.

Jakob laughs and strokes the dog.

(They met when he attended a lecture series she presented on invertebrates, and became friends afterwards.)

When not talking, they sit in companionable silence. These long breaks in conversation make her even more conscious of the silence. But now silence is not unpleasant. Jakob drinks his tea and absent-mindedly strokes the dog.

He's also read, he says, that there are no shadows on the sun. A deafening roar of raw power rages ceaselessly in a blaze of utter silence, he quotes.

She senses it: The silence of the universe has now come to nest in her house. She feels this silence in her every cell.

For the rest of the week she is constantly aware of this silence. (Not even the croaking of a frog – it's too dry for that.) How is it possible that the evenings are so long when Willem isn't here? How is it possible that this neighbourhood is so quiet? Apart from the dogs barking, not a sound. Why doesn't it strike her more often? Because she gets distracted by Willem's presence?

The dog's head is resting on her front paws, sometimes with her eyes open. Is she thinking of him? What does he mean to her? In the evening silence the only sound is the dog lying on the sofa and sometimes licking her paw. Perhaps the dog is depressed, perhaps she's bored, perhaps she's missing Willem. Even when she's asleep, her ears are pricked up. She picks up sounds that Magrieta is unaware of. Magrieta also misses Willem. Without his steadying presence she feels like a bobbing leaf. She misses the soft skin of his neck, the instep of his foot, his intimate, defensive look. She almost lost him when she burnt all her bridges behind her, when the skull was her banner and the reign of death her blazon; when Kali the Terrible was her guiding principle. She is aware of the night behind the windows. She bears in mind the great distance between here and the mountain. She thinks it is important to position herself constantly in relation to the earthworm, the mountain, and her husband.

Once again she is taken by surprise by a WhatsApp from her daughter. I think of you, the girl writes, I think of you all the time, actually. But if I don't shut myself off from you, to a degree, I'll never find my feet here. It's difficult, because I miss you a lot.

*

Magrieta receives a WhatsApp from Isabel: *Any news of Mister Fire Eyes?*

No, Magrieta replies, *nothing yet. But I'm on his case.* She has to laugh. Mister Fire Eyes. Potsdam does indeed have remarkable eyes, such a glowing deep brown, just a pity he has such difficulty making eye contact.

In the office by day, with Isabel up North and Markus Potsdam God knows where, the silence susurrates without mercy. She sits in her office, she looks at the mountains. The silence surges against her eardrums. At times it feels as if Potsdam is more present in his absence than he was in his presence. Fucking mysterious, she thinks, the situation with the man. And fucking frustrating, because the work's piling up, she only just manages to get it done on her own.

Thirteen

One morning, in the middle of the following week (neither Willem nor Isabel is back yet), Bertie Oberholzer turns up on her doorstep at the Bureau again. There he stands, once again in boots, shorts and red-and-white checked shirt, clearly impervious to the cold. Her heart sinks into her shoes. He is the last person on earth she has strength to see today. (It is the end of August, but still bitterly cold. In the office by day it is as quiet as in the house by night. The silence here feels to her as violent as at home – like an onslaught on her inner ear, as if it's compressing her lungs.) Something about him is different today. It takes her a few moments to register that he is clean-shaven. Not a single hair left on his face – beard, moustache, sideburns, everything off, everything except his heavy eyebrows. His clean-shaven face looks smaller without the hair. The shaven skin looks tender, red, raw. Without the facial hair he looks less simian, less threatening, more defenceless. More unguarded.

May he come in for a moment? (She hopes he's not going to continue his tirade against Deneys Swiegers. She's not in a sympathetic mood.)

But no, this morning he is not on about Swiegers. He wants to say something about Markus Potsdam. They were at high school together in Vredenburg on the West Coast. His parents live in Jameson Bay, in fact. (Jameson Bay, where the fish washed up – how is it possible that Potsdam didn't mention it?) They weren't friends. Markus was two or three years ahead of him. He was very clever. Brilliant. He was the cleverest child in the whole history of the school. He was good at sports too. Markus was his hero. He admired him boundlessly. They didn't have contact at university either. Then Markus left, overseas. Cambridge or somewhere. And it's not true, says Bertie Oberholzer (his face red with embarrassment), they did not play chess together. It's true that they were in the school chess team together, but they never played chess together in later years. He's very sorry that he misled Magrieta. He doesn't know what got into him. He actually knows very little about Markus Potsdam. He also had no contact with him later, after university. (The sore, raw skin of his face flushes even redder after this admission.) He only heard about him again when Swiegers started doing work for the Bureau. He doesn't think Markus would even know who he is.

For a few moments Magrieta sits speechless, just looking at the man.

Why didn't he say so from the start? Why come up with the story of Kogelberg? she asks.

He doesn't know, says Bertie. He was caught on the back foot. He didn't want to say too much in front of Swiegers. Whatever he says, Swiegers always uses it against him.

And the blue house?

That is true. He once heard from his sister, who has a friend in Kogelberg, that Markus has a house there. A blue house. His sister was friendly with someone who knew Markus at school. But he thinks they also lost touch a long time ago.

'What else?' Magrieta asks.

'That's all,' says Bertie, sheepishly.

'Is he or has he ever been married?'

'I don't know.'

Because Bertie Oberholzer is looking close to tears again, she suggests that they should have coffee in the coffee shop on the floor below the Bureau. Bertie is glad, even touched.

Unfortunately he can't be too long, says Bertie, Swiegers doesn't know he's gone. Magrieta, anxious that he might start expounding on Swiegers again, thanks Bertie warmly for the information, stresses how she appreciates his frankness, asks if he could perhaps find out where

Potsdam's parents live in Jameson Bay, and starts diplomatically walking him to the exit. He'll try to find out for her whether they are still in their old house, he promises. He undertakes, in fact, to do everything in his power to gather information about Markus.

Well, well, well, she thinks, *that* she didn't expect! Potsdam's parents live in Jameson Bay, he grew up there, but – as was to be expected – he made no mention of this when he sent Magrieta there at the beginning of the year to meet the asthmatic agent. The agent who then unfortunately died in his hotel room in Cape Town. What the true state of affairs was, why she had to meet the agent, whether Potsdam had anything out of the ordinary up his sleeve, that she'll never know. Except if Potsdam, if and when he ever returns, spills the whole bushel of beans. Not exactly the kind of frankness of temperament that she's come to associate with him.

*

On Saturday evening Magrieta takes an Uber back from Cape Town. She's attended an all-day conference on the development of administrative skills. It was dead boring and a waste of time. It was sheer torture, from beginning to end. What am I *doing* here, she kept thinking. She didn't feel like taking her own car, because then she couldn't drink, but her forethought turned out to be wasted, because at lunch there was no sign of alcohol.

To her surprise the driver of the Uber is a woman, a tall, thin woman with short, dark hair. The woman wants to talk, but Magrieta is not in the mood. She's talked enough for one day, she's exhausted, she's frustrated, she's in a hurry to get home. May she ask what Magrieta was doing in Cape Town? asks the woman. Work-related matters, says Magrieta, these days more than her pound of flesh is demanded of her. On the passenger seat next to the woman is a book. Magrieta doesn't feel like a sustained conversation, but she does ask the woman what she's reading.

The new novel by Michel Houellebecq. Houellebecq is indescribably ugly, says the woman, he complains about older women whose every feature sags and droops, but he himself looks like a withered sexual organ. Does she read while she's working, then, Magrieta asks. Oh, she sometimes has to wait for a client, and she likes always having a book at hand. But even when she's not reading, she usually has a lot to think about.

The woman switches on the radio. The Saturday evening request programme has just started. At first Magrieta wants to ask the woman to switch it off, but then thinks it can't do any harm as a little exercise in nostalgia. They listened to this programme regularly as a family on Saturday evenings. Friday evenings were good, Saturday evenings were good. Sunday evenings were dreadful. She sometimes went to sleep in church with her head on her mother's shoulder. She hated church and she hated school. She knows that as a child she was dealt a grievous blow by the combination of church and school, with Sunday school the final tribulation. Never has she been as forlorn as one morning when she had to walk to Sunday school on her own, in tears. Her mother at home as implacable as the fiery angel at the gates of paradise.

A short distance after the turn-off from the N2 onto Baden Powell Drive, in the area where the prostitutes normally ply their trade, there is clearly something happening – a protest action of some kind, with burning tyres and branches in the road. The usual scenario. Once again a stop-go situation, as during the protest action on the way to the airport. Magrieta is impatient, the last thing on earth she has the patience for now is having to sit and wait on this godforsaken plain. It must be the most cheerless place between here and Cape Town, and the water purification plant also stinks to high heaven.

Talita Sonnekus has just requested 'Beautiful Isle of Somewhere' for her friends Santie, Ina, Markus and Paulus in Westonaria.

'My *fuck*,' says the woman, 'it's the whores who are protesting!'

And indeed, some distance ahead of them, on the strip of grass on the left-hand side of the road, it is clear that there are women protest-ing. Although it's dark and there are quite a few cars ahead of them, a few drums filled with burning coals plus the lights of the waiting vehicles illuminate the scene well enough to make out what's happening. From where they're sitting, they can see some of the women closest to them – a fair amount of flesh is on display, a fair amount of thigh and a fair amount of breast – most of them dressed in skimpy skirts or hotpants with bare midriffs. Working clothes. On some of the placards they can make out *Better working conditions, We want better protection, Free medi-cal care, Where is our Union, Legalise our trade, Stop abuse against women.* A few who are not holding placards are dancing and singing around the fire.

The Slave Chorus from *Nabucco* by Verdi is next in line. It has been requested by Marinda de Lange for her parents-in-law, brother-in-law and sister-in-law in Port Elizabeth.

'Why are they protesting at night?' asks the Uber woman.

'I suppose they work during the day,' says Magrieta.

'I thought prostitutes were mainly night workers.'

'There are always a few here during the day,' says Magrieta. 'And the night shift is probably imminent. As soon as they're done here.'

'I suppose the pimps are hiding in the bushes,' says the woman.

'The pimps and the impatient clients. Or they're lying under the bridge, there's not a bush in sight here.'

'On blow-up mattresses.'

'I doubt it.'

Magrieta has never seen such a large gathering of prostitutes – nei-ther here nor elsewhere. (Not even on television.) The women usually sit here on their own, sometimes two or three together. She finds it appal-ling when she drives past – the sickening smell that hangs in this area, the barren landscape, the women who have to sit here all day, on a very hot day often on a rock, in only the meagre shade of a Port Jackson tree. Inconceivably barren. Inconceivably desolate, upsetting, but also intriguing. What does such a woman think, sitting here all day on a rock? Sometimes, when there are more than one, they plait each other's hair.

On the other side of the road there's also something happening. Two cars have pulled off the road and a few young men are shouting remarks at the women across the road. Judging by their body language, they are taunting the women. Clearly a great joke to them. Somebody must have spread the word that there was a cool event happening – an opportunity for some fun. They seem to be all white, all young. Difficult to see them properly in the dark.

'Trust the fucking whites to make a joke of this,' says the Uber woman.

The woman sits in front. Magrieta sits in the back. On the radio, the oldest Afrikaans radio programme. It's a clear night. A night of fireworks and shooting stars. The indifferent and expanding universe is doing its thing – it expands; supernovas explode; two gravitational eddies collide with each other, which releases inconceivably large amounts of energy. Photons surge inexorably from the core of the sun to its surface (it can take up to a million years). Here, on earth – briefer than the blink of an eye in the cosmos – something exceptional is happening tonight. Completely unique, unless our earth and our universe is one of innumerable identical earths and universes.

Richard Tauber is up next with 'Adieu, mein kleiner Gardeoffizier'. This is the request of Herman and Nakkie Pelser of Somerset West for their parents and parents-in-law from Heilbron in the Free State.

The stop-and-go takes exceptionally long tonight because there are quite a few cars coming from the front, moving very slowly through the obstacles in the road. The Uber woman winds down her window. What the men are shouting at the women is not clearly audible, but some of the women are more than ready to join in. They shout back. In the light of the flames the women look voluptuous, and they make quite a show of provocative movements, which spurs on the men across the road to probably greater obscenities. One of the men runs forward and performs a very unambiguous obscene movement with his hips. Behind him the others can themselves laughing.

At last Magrieta and the woman can also go. Because the prostitutes are close to the side of the road, they get a good view of them. They drive past so slowly that one of the women in passing presses her face close to Magrieta's window and yells something, she is so close to the car that Magrieta can clearly see her red mouth and abundant breasts; she's wearing skin-tight purple leggings that clearly delineate her thighs. She shouts something, but Magrieta can't make out what she's saying.

'Shall I wind down the window and extend the hand of friendship?' she asks.

'It's probably too late,' says the Uber woman.

As they drive past, the woman slaps the roof twice in quick succession. Magrieta looks at her own arm. When she tilts her palm up, the blue veins are visible in her forearm. Richard Tauber sings with great feeling and abandon, Adieu, adieu. Should she ask the Uber woman to stop, let her get out, leave the security of her car (and, indeed, of her house and her white entitlement), stagger in among the protesting women, declare herself and say: I am on your side, my heart bleeds for those who are exploited and humiliated every day? Should she try to overcome the ignominious distance between herself and the disenfranchised, as the woman in the vineyard was planning to do in her last days? Perhaps not the woman's last days, but her last days in the vineyard. Her disappearance remains mystifying. Greater sacrifices are now called for. Greater renunciations. Less of one thing and more of another. God knows it's complex. Or no. Maybe it's quite simple. Off with the blinkers! Away with denial!

The 'Elizabeth Serenade' is up next, requested by Poppie Griesel for her brother Joppie in the Strand and for her friend Karlien in Bredasdorp. Magrieta and the woman's eyes meet in the rear-view mirror; her gaze is dark, ironic.

'They've been playing the "Elizabeth Serenade" on this programme every Saturday night for the last seventy years,' says Magrieta.

'I know,' says the woman, 'and they'll be doing it for the next seventy years as well.'

'Until it's the last remaining Afrikaans programme.'

'And it's presented in English.'

'I'll be pushing up daisies by then, thank God,' says Magrieta.

'All of us,' says the woman.

'The sooner the better,' says Magrieta. Perhaps she and her compatriots should crawl back into the sea, like the first amphibian life forms, to evolve all over again into more compassionate life forms.

Her eye catches the woman's once more when Willem Pelser reads out the next request: Brahms' *Academic Festival Overture* for Irma Hanekom of Vereeniging. She is requesting it for her friends Petrus and Hantie of Florida.

'The *Academic Festival Overture*,' says the woman, 'spot-on. I couldn't have requested anything more appropriate myself.'

When they're well on their way to Stellenbosch again, the woman introduces herself as Alta Meyer. She does the Uber thing purely for her own pleasure, she says. In this way she gets to meet interesting characters. And it gets her out of the house, which she hates and despises. The house cramps her style, not that she has all that much style to cramp. She doesn't do the Uber thing every day, only when she feels the need for something else, twice, three times a week. And it's her own car, she deducts it from tax.

They reach the end of the request programme with 'One Fine Day' from *Madama Butterfly* by Puccini, for Nettie and Koos of Kroonstad.

She thought Kroonstad had been depopulated of all whites, says Alta.

She wouldn't know, says Magrieta. She's not been paying attention of late.

No water, says Alta. Shit situation. The privileged have water flown in. Those without the means, she doesn't know how they manage.

'What is the government doing?'

'Nothing.'

Magrieta looks to the left. A dam, half-full. 'The drought continues,' she says.

'Yes. It's God punishing the country for the sins of the past and the transgressions of the present.'

'I met somebody who said that God should wipe out the Afrikaners for their attitude to evolution and gays,' says Magrieta. 'The woman threw away her cellphone and pitched a tent in a vineyard near my house.'

'That sounds like a plan,' says Alta.

'She wanted to escape her life.'

'She should have joined the Uber fleet.'

'Too late now. When I went back, she was gone. No sign of the tent either. My husband helped me look. Later the police as well.'

'No body found?'

'No.'

'Hectic.'

'Yes. I suppose so.'

'Enough about me. What do *you* do for a living?'

'I should be doing research into the nervous system of the phylum Annelida from the Ordovician – the earthworm, actually – but for the past year or so I've been attached to a bureau for continuing education. The Cape branch of the bureau.'

In the rear-view mirror the woman seems interested.

'Earthworms?' she asks.

'Yes,' says Magrieta.

'I know nothing about geological eras, but they interest me. Ordovician?'

'It started about 485 million years ago. Lasted about 45 million years. Lukewarm seas, little happening on dry land, just about all life in the oceans. Earth was bombarded by asteroids at that time. The period starts and ends with great extinctions. An ice age at the end. Above the equator there were mainly oceans, the lower land mass was what we call Gondwana.'

'So life began in the sea?'

'More or less, yes. Greenhouse-like conditions are characteristic of the period, but the Late Ordovician is one of the coldest periods in the last 600 million years of the earth's history.'

'Heavens,' says the woman.

'Tropical life forms were hit hard by the first wave of extinctions, cold water species during the second.'

'Extinctions,' says the woman, 'of what kind?'

'One theory is that the earth was struck by a ten-second gamma-ray explosion. That would have destroyed the ozone layer, exposed land and sea life to fatal radiation and caused the ice age.'

'A ten-second gamma-ray explosion is all it takes?'

'Yes,' says Magrieta. 'It depends how strong it is. Even a lighter explosion would cause an instant stoppage of all power on earth. No communication of any kind possible – no internet, no telephone, no cellphone, radio, nothing. No heating. No food. No water. No transport. Nothing. Absolutely nothing. Only the sun by day and the pitch darkness at night. Large-scale plundering. You can imagine it. No medical services, no medicine. Essential foodstuffs become unavailable. Food rots in the shops. People start robbing and murdering each other.'

'Cannibalism.'

'That is certainly a possibility. Plagues and epidemics too, of which cholera is one of the more pleasant options.'

'The apocalypse interests me,' says Alta Meyer. 'I've suffered from insomnia ever since I was five. So I've spent many hours at night thinking up end-of-time scenarios. Starting with Revelations. The Whore arising from the sea. There's always been enough material to feed even the feeblest imagination.'

'Yes, indeed.' (Apocalypse fatigue, the woman in the vineyard said.)

They drive on in silence for a while.

'Do you think there is life elsewhere in the universe,' asks the woman, 'specifically places where things are less shit than here?'

'Definitely,' says Magrieta, 'but the universe is too big for us ever to know. There must be millions of worlds that can sustain life. But the origin of life is in all probability an arduous process. Very erratic. The evolution of intelligence also. And then, to develop the necessary technology to travel intergalactically and further, perhaps even more difficult.'

'Bummer,' says the woman.

'Yes, isn't it.'

'So much for the Biblical promise that now we see through a glass darkly, but one day face to face.'

'Indeed,' says Magrieta (who laments the fact that, unlike God, she does not have an overview of the inception and evolution of all of creation – from the Big Bang to today).

Alta shrugs. 'I'm gradually scaling down any expectations I ever had of anything. Seeing face to face heads the list.'

Magrieta laughs softly in the back of the car. 'Yes, indeed,' she says.

As they drive past Soverby on the Annandale Road, Alta Meyer says: 'A friend of mine is here this weekend with a bottle of whisky and a few crime novels.'

Through the window Magrieta sees the dark shapes of cows in a field, and she knows there are marsh roses twining up the fence. Perhaps she wasted her time with worms. She could have been a better-rounded person.

'He shouldn't be drinking,' says Alta, 'he's a rehabilitated alcoholic.'

'Should we go and deliver him from his folly?'

'He won't appreciate it.'

Shortly thereafter Alta Meyer drops her at home. Phone any time you want transport, she says, and hands Magrieta her card.

*

Willem returns the next day. His mother's condition has stabilised. The minor unpleasantness after her return from Albany West in abeyance (they haven't yet spoken about it again). Magrieta lies in his arms that evening (safe, she thinks, for the time being safe again from apocalypse and worse). He tells her about a dream he had the previous night. (It's unusual for Willem to tell her his dreams. It's not that he doesn't dream, it's just that he doesn't believe in inflicting your dreams on other people. She's always been grateful to him for that.) But this dream clearly upset him, or confused him, or he finds it cryptic. Under his T-shirt or shirt there is a small leguaan sitting upright. He can't feel it and he can't see it either, but he knows it's there. Then a larger leguaan comes in from outside, with a tongue that flickers like a snake's forked tongue. He doesn't know if the larger leguaan is coming to attack or protect the little one. Eventually it turns out that he and the big leguaan, or lizard, will keep the little one warm.

It's a dream about you and your father and death, says Magrieta.

Fourteen

Spring arrives. Everywhere new leaves appear. But an unusually dry summer, following on the dry winter, is forecast.

Bertie Oberholzer comes to visit Magrieta again at the Bureau office. He's found out that Markus Potsdam's parents are still living in Jameson Bay, and he has their address for her. They still run the shop in the town. He doesn't know how much contact Markus still has with his parents, but at least it's a starting point. She thanks him warmly for the information.

He doesn't get up. She can see he still has something on his mind.

'What is it, Bertie?' she asks.

'It's Swiegers,' he says.

'What is it this time?'

'He doesn't treat me well. He doesn't respect me. There are many things . . . that I can't talk about.'

'With the duck?'

'With the duck, yes, but not only with the duck.'

'With what, then?' she asks.

'You don't have any *idea*,' he says, suddenly vehement. (He's said that before.)

'No,' she says, 'because you're not telling me.'

'He's going to regret it bitterly. Bitterly!'

'Bertie,' she says, 'do you ever talk to Swiegers about these things bothering you?'

'Talk?!' Bertie says, with a small, sardonic smile.

'Yes, talk.'

'If only one could talk to Deneys!' he says, with a bitter grimace.

When it seems as if he's set to stay much longer, she thanks him

warmly once again for the Potsdams' address and manoeuvres him tactfully out of the office.

Later that week she drops in on Deneys Swiegers for Bureau matters.
She likes to see how the duck is progressing. She finds the laboratory
space familiar; it relaxes her. The only dissonant chord here is Bertie
Oberholzer, who, on her every visit, puts his head around the door with
frustrating regularity, to alert Deneys to something or other – as he does
once again today. He greets Magrieta curtly (no indication that they
have quite recently had a personal conversation), and asks Swiegers how
far he is – there are students waiting to see him. It's urgent. Just a moment,
says Swiegers calmly, he won't be long.

'What's the matter with Bertie?' Magrieta asks cautiously. 'He doesn't
seem to like me being here.'

Swiegers utters a chuckle. 'Well, old Bertie,' he says amiably, 'he's
inclined to get worked up about everything. He can make things unnecessarily difficult for himself at times.'

'Such as?' Magrieta asks.

'Petty things. But he needs to stop delaying and finish his thesis
now. He's dawdling too long over it. It's spoiling his chances of pro-
motion in the department.'

'So is he ambitious?' Magrieta asks.

'Yes and no,' says Swiegers. 'But he can turn very bitter when he feels
he's been wronged. He feels, for instance, that I should give him more
credit for his share in the duck.'

'His share?'

'With the programming. But he's never going to find *any* credit
sufficient.'

While he's talking, she's checking Swiegers out surreptitiously. *That*
innocent he can't be either. Behind that open boyish face and clear eyes
there may well be hiding an obstinacy that can be moved by neither
heaven nor earth. The man must have some part in Bertie's unhappi-
ness – surely he can't be imagining *all* of it. Deneys strokes the soft latex

surface of the mechanical duck (as she likes to refer to it) far too possessively. She knows what bitter fights academics can have over intellectual property. But she's inclined to stay out of this. They'll have to battle out their shares in the programming of the duck between the two of them. She does not – like Solomon with the two women and the child – want to be part of their tug-of-war about it. She doesn't want to be a shoulder for Bertie to cry on any more either.

She's annoyed, because Bertie's regular interruptions are starting to get on her nerves and making her want to get away, whereas she'd actually like to talk to Deneys about the future of technological developments, like the escalating use of machines and algorithms, in connection with a book she's recently read on the subject – a very dystopian vision of the future. A book in which it is argued that only the super-rich will ultimately benefit from all the new technologies, while the masses, shut off, will pursue the illusion of happiness through drugs and virtual reality.

*

Isabel is back. Magrieta realises how much she's missed the young woman's unruffled presence. How lovely she is, with her soft pale skin and cool grey eyes, and long, slow limbs. Magrieta is grateful that the silence, which was threatening to press the air out of her lungs, has been broken.

She tells Isabel that she's been given an address for Potsdam's parents by Bertie Oberholzer. Isabel won't believe it, but they live in Jameson Bay. She thought of phoning first, but now she's decided she's just going to visit them direct.

'Fuck a buck,' says the girl.

'I know you think I'm being silly,' says Magrieta, 'but for as long as I don't know where Potsdam is and how he is, my hands are tied. They're tied anyway.'

'I told you from the outset that you should be looking for another job,' says Isabel.

'What do you think I'm doing? There's nothing, believe me.'

Isabel looks sceptical. 'Don't worry too much about Potsdam. He's okay,' she says.

'I thought you said he walked into the sea.'

'Yes, but he may have washed up again.'

'Do you have another hunch?'

'You could say that, yes.'

'You're just saying that to put my mind at ease.'

'Okay, if you think so.'

'What else should I think?'

'Relax. Don't stop looking for something else.'

'And if I do find something and he's not back yet?'

'Then you lock the Bureau door and post the key to headquarters.'

Fifteen

Magrieta girds her loins and prepares herself for a second visit to Jameson Bay. She reckons it's improbable that Potsdam's parents won't know where or how he is – possible, but improbable. She says goodbye to Willem, who thinks she's being silly. He wants to advise her in no uncertain terms to let the whole Potsdam affair go, it's actually getting a bit ridiculous, she does realise that, doesn't she? And he can guarantee her now already that nothing will come of it, but he knows she won't listen to him, once she's got her mind set on something there's no getting her off it. He's seen the fanatical glint in her eye of late.

This time she goes on her own. She decides to stay in the hotel, just the *thought* of the guesthouse on the hill, with the memory of her pain and extreme physical discomfort, gives her the heebie-jeebies. Also the mere thought of the aniseed rusks they bought at the farm stall makes her nauseous in advance.

So it's the town hotel, and that at the Bureau's expense, because it's on account of Potsdam's irresponsible behaviour that she's here. (Perhaps she *is* being a bit ridiculous. But she has a plan, and she's sticking to it.)

She arrives in Jameson Bay in the late afternoon. On their previous visit they hadn't seen much of the town apart from the fish-and-chips shop and the beach on which the whale had washed up and the dead man had lain under the blanket. Whereas it's actually a very attractive coastal village, still relatively unspoilt, with a character of its own. But after her fall there had hardly been time to explore the village and surrounds. There are several shops in the main street, a library, a few eating places, a home industry, a Wimpy, a Standard Bank, a church, and a large general dealer – Potsdam & Sons.

Was it expected of Markus to stand behind the counter, along with his brothers? She can hardly picture him behind a counter, bolts of cloth on a shelf behind him. Perhaps his brilliance exempted him from his share in the family business.

She likes the hotel. Elegant, in an old-world way. Beautiful old building. Lovely wrought-iron balustrade in the foyer leading to the first floor. Something grand, European, about the feel of the place. It wouldn't surprise her if it also belonged to the Potsdams. She likes her room, it is spacious and cool.

*

That evening she eats in the hotel dining room – a large room, with wood panelling on the walls. There are not many guests. Two families at two separate tables, at the table behind her a man sitting on his own. An elderly couple in one corner, three women at another table covertly regarding her with interest. And in the furthest corner, another man on his own, dressed in a bulky black overcoat, although it's not particularly cold.

It was dumb of them not to stay in the hotel on their previous visit. It would have been so much better. And much closer to the sea. If they'd stayed here, she wouldn't have fallen. If she hadn't fallen, she wouldn't have been dosed with all that medicine by the quack. If she hadn't been in a befuddled state when she looked at the whale, would there still have been that slight shift in her head? If everything had been different, perhaps the mysterious asthmatic agent wouldn't have died in his hotel room the evening before their meeting.

But here she sits, now, and for the first time in a long while she feels at peace. It's a relief to be away from the Bureau, even for a short while. With Potsdam gone, she and Isabel have had to work twice as hard (even though according to her he only sat in his office playing sudoku). Between the fish course and the main course she thinks of hotel dining rooms on seaside holidays with her parents. The fish tasted *exactly* like this, and there was always white bread with the soup. Mornings on the beach, and sometimes she and her brother played with other children in the hotel in the evenings; rode up and down in the lifts once, she remembers.

There is suddenly a commotion at the main entrance. Five people in wheelchairs enter the dining room, with considerable moving of tables and chairs and manoeuvring on the part of the staff to get them all seated at the nearest table. A serious gathering, by the looks of it. All men. All robust of upper body. And they are all wearing black T-shirts, with a small logo on the left breast. It takes quite a while for them to settle to the point where they can start eating.

Good heavens, she can't turn her back in a strange place without a person in a wheelchair appearing, on his own or as part of a convention or delegation or whatever else.

She asks the waitress serving her whether she knows what the people in wheelchairs are doing here in town, is there perhaps a gathering or something, but the woman has no idea either. Magrieta involuntarily thinks of the unpleasant Agent Oliver, on his Kindle in the coffee shop, and the fellow who almost flattened her and a crowd of other people in the centre of town, shortly after her meeting with said agent. Ever since her meeting with the fascist Oliver she has been less well disposed to wheelchair users, or is at least distrustful of them. And then of course the terrorist group in the novel she once read. Horrendously violent. Wheelchair terrorists. The black T-shirts (illegibly small logo) are not a good sign. Hangmen? Funeral directors? Don't be silly, she chides herself, but what if it's true, or worse. She watches the group at the table closely to see if she can deduce anything regarding their agenda.

But hardly have the wheelchair group started eating their soup, with evident gusto, when the manager enters the dining room. He is so sorry to disturb, but would the guests please leave the room immediately, one and all, a strange suitcase has been found in the entrance foyer. No cause for panic (already the first signs of this among the guests), it's just to ensure their safety, only until the police have investigated the matter. Nothing to be concerned about, he assures them, although he looks thoroughly panic-stricken himself. Would everybody please proceed to the side veranda through the side doors.

Light hysteria. The families gather their children to their breasts. What about our cameras and valuables upstairs in our rooms? one of the women asks. One of the children starts crying. The manager requests that the wheelchair group be allowed to leave the room first. With great agility the chaps move out between the tables, while the guests regard them with barely concealed resentment (if there is a bomb in the case, it stands to reason that people in wheelchairs have less to lose). As soon as the group have left by the side door the rest of the guests clump out after them. Everybody huddles together on the wide side stoep overlooking the sea. Magrieta takes care to sit near to the group, to watch them from close by and to get a clearer view of the logo. But she is just not close enough, in the press of people and the bad light, to see what the logo represents. It's a beautiful evening. The sea is as flat as a sheet of glass. Phosphorus on the breakers. A police siren comes into earshot soon afterwards. Everyone sits, tense and waiting. Not much is said, beyond a largely subdued whispering.

After about half an hour the manager comes to call them back in. The wheelchair group are allowed to re-enter the room first. After that the rest of the guests resume their seats at their respective tables. Nothing further to be concerned about, the manager assures them, the police have left with the suspect case. Drinks on the house, and milkshakes for the children. He apologises copiously. You can never be too careful these days, he says. There has recently been unrest in the township outside the town. You never know with these people, he says, there are so many criminal elements among them. This he says while the coloured waitress, waiting for him to stop talking, stands next to him with expressionless face and a laden tray.

The man who was sitting at the table behind her asks Magrieta if he can join her. Before she can consent, he has already taken a seat opposite hers. A sly grin, hideous hairstyle, and a dark, sparse moustache and beard. (A double for Billy Bob Thornton in the television series *Fargo*.) And what brings her to their pretty little town? Oh, she's come to enjoy the sea air and the solitude, she says pointedly.

He leans over to her confidentially. It *was* a bomb, he says, it wasn't just a false alarm. The manager has just confirmed it. He glances over his shoulder conspiratorially. For the benefit of the guests the man will deny it, of course, he says. Nobody likes the idea of a bomb in the hotel they're staying in.

'Do they know who it is?' she asks. 'Has anyone accepted responsibility?'

'No,' he says, wipes the corners of his mouth with his napkin, and puts his hand out across the table. 'Donald Dippenaar, attorney, of Dippenaar and Dolfuss, pleased to meet you.'

He can clearly not *wait* to spill his story. He's new in town. He's just opened a practice here. He decided to exchange his successful practice in the city for something smaller, the pressure of such a large practice had become *just* too much.

Charlatan, Magrieta thinks, like the quack doctor who treated her, who couldn't make the grade in the competitive city environment and now wants to come and exploit the poor small-town people and holidaymakers.

You wouldn't think so, he continues, but there's plenty of internecine tension in such a small place – factions, infighting. Racial tension, of course, there is plenty of. Alcohol and drug abuse among the young people in the adjoining township. Unemployment. Every social evil you can think of. As an attorney you see *everything*, he says with unabashed pride.

Oh yes? says Magrieta. She knows he wants her to ask him about the *everything* he's seen, but she doesn't want to give him the satisfaction of questioning him.

Has he made the acquaintance yet of the Potsdam family in town? she asks.

'The Jews?' he asks. 'No, they keep themselves to themselves, mix only with their own kind. The Jews are after all an inbred race, with all their intermarriage.'

'The Jews are not a race,' says Magrieta, 'they're an ethnic group and they don't intermarry.'

And looking at some Afrikaners, she adds, fixing him with a stare, *they* seem pretty inbred to her. (Jews? She should have known, she didn't think of the possibility – how stupid of her; she should have known – the unusual surname and the singularly dark eyes and beard. But Markus Potsdam is so fluently Afrikaans in speech and sense of humour that the possibility never occurred to her.)

This admonition, though, makes little impression on Donald Dippenaar. But an interesting case, he says, and once again leans forward conspiratorially, is the guy diagonally behind him in the corner, and he points with his eyes in the direction of the man in the black coat sitting on his own at a table. The fellow is reputedly stinking rich, he reputedly lives on a farm just outside the town, but a weirdo, reputedly he does tricks with knives. Tricks of what kind? she asks, reluctant to admit that she's interested. Oh, of that he's not sure. He thinks the fellow throws knives at the Fishbone Restaurant. And reputedly he rents himself out for parties. Weirdos, he says, a town full of weirdos.

Of which you clearly are one, she thinks. And the group in wheelchairs, she asks, does he have any idea what they're doing here, she couldn't make out the logo on their T-shirts.

Oh, he's not sure, he thinks they have something to do with whales. But he's not sure.

With whales?! Magrieta exclaims.

The man looks at her askance for a moment. Tilts his head slightly sideways, like a dog hearing a suspicious sound. He has small pupils, like those of a swindler – two vicious black specks like the points of a dagger. Nothing big-hearted about this man, he'll screw you over properly if you don't watch out.

Yes, whales, if he got it right, but he's not exactly sure what.

Magrieta has all of a sudden had enough of this smug attorney's little stories. She gets up so abruptly that she almost upsets her chair.

When she moves past the group in wheelchairs on the way out, she tries to make out the logo on the chest of the one closest to her. She can't believe it – unless she's sorely mistaken, it is the same pictogram as the one behind the toilet doors months ago!

She stops dead in her tracks, and asks the man closest to her what the logo on his shirt represents. May she have a look? Certainly, he says. On a closer look, she sees that it's similar enough, but not quite the same – the whale emblem is a mite clearer. And may she ask what they're doing in the town? Oh yes, they belong to the Association of Friends of the Whale.

Oh, Magrieta exclaims enthusiastically, that sounds interesting! How does one go about joining this group, she has a very special (she wants to say bond, but checks herself) interest in whales.

The speaker hesitates for a moment before saying: Unfortunately the group is not for everyone.

Of course, she should have taken into account that they're all in wheelchairs.

And what does the group *do*? she asks. Suddenly conscious of the fact that owing to her height she is towering above the seated men, which must be even worse for them because she's a woman.

The man hesitates again, glances uncertainly at the rest of the group for a few moments and says: They don't really like divulging their activities to just anyone. It's sort of –

'Secret?!' Magrieta exclaims. She looks at one face after the other – each member of the group is looking at her attentively. 'A secret organisation calling themselves friends of the whale? Something like the Freemasons, but with a greener agenda?'

'Not exactly *secret*, no,' says the official spokesperson, clearly offended, 'and also not an organisation that is in *any* way comparable to the Freemasons!'

'Of course,' says Magrieta, 'sorry – I realise your activities are none of my business. Sorry!' And with that she leaves the dining room, considerably embarrassed and with burning cheeks.

*

Tomorrow she's going to visit Markus' parents. She has no idea what she'll find there. So little could she imagine him, up to now, in any parental or family relation, indeed in any context other than in front of his computer at the Bureau, with the shirt always straining across his shoulders.

*

The next morning she finds Markus' parental home without any difficulty. It is in the older, more established part of town, two streets from the sea. A big old house, with wide verandas all the way around. It must have been one of the first houses built here, she guesses.

She knocks with a beating heart. She didn't notify the people that she'd be coming. A domestic helper with a white apron and head wrap opens the door. She'll call Mrs Potsdam.

The mother is a small woman. Sympathetic face. Markus' eyes. Magrieta introduces herself as Markus' colleague from the Bureau. She's visiting the town; Markus said that if she was ever in the vicinity she should come by (white lie; the last thing on earth Markus Potsdam would ever say, he'd likely disapprove very strongly of her visit).

Mrs Potsdam puts her hand on her heart. 'How is he?' she asks anxiously. (Then they have probably not had recent contact with him either.)

She invites Magrieta in cordially. Come in, have a seat. Tea or coffee? The sitting room is large, cool, dusky, elegant in an old-world way.

'Markus is not at work at the moment,' Magrieta says. 'He's taken leave for a while.'

Mrs Potsdam nods. She's clearly eager to hear more about him. 'It's good to meet someone who works with him,' she says, 'we hear from him so seldom these days.'

'Markus is doing well at the Bureau,' says Magrieta (now she must be careful what she says). 'He's a competent manager. The Bureau is doing good work under his management.'

'Competent Markus certainly is,' says the mother, 'very competent,' and she looks down at her lap. When she looks up, her eyes are filled with tears.

'We are sometimes worried about him,' she says. 'He struggles at times . . . and he took the death of his cousin so hard.'

'His cousin?' Magrieta asks.

'His cousin who died so unexpectedly at the beginning of the year in Cape Town. A nephew of my husband. Ever since childhood they've been inseparable. Like David and Jonathan.'

'The asthma sufferer?' Magrieta asks, startled.

The mother nods. 'It couldn't have been easy for him,' she says again, softly.

The asthmatic agent. The man she referred to in her conversation with Markus as the asthmatic agent. So belittling. She's ashamed of her comment. Without any inkling that it could perhaps be someone close to Markus. The man she was supposed to meet here in Jameson Bay. For what purpose? Could Markus not just have said it was his cousin, couldn't he have said why Magrieta had to meet him here, in the same town where his parents live? It could hardly have been work-related.

She's now completely thrown. Fortunately at this point the servant brings the tray with coffee. Fragrant coffee and home-baked apple strudel. Magrieta is grateful for the opportunity to recover from her dismay.

How long have they been living here? she asks. Oh, many years, says the mother. Practically since they opened the shop. But her husband retired recently. Markus' eldest brother, Ezra, is now managing the shop.

Was she born here? Magrieta asks cautiously. Oh yes, she was born South African, she's from Vredenburg. She met her husband here. Before her marriage – she makes a slight hand gesture – she adopted the faith. His parents came to South Africa from Germany in 1938, just before the war. The rest of their family – his parents' brothers and sisters – stayed behind. They were not so lucky. They all perished, she says softly. Samuel's parents went to the Transvaal. They settled there. Samuel and his brothers were born there. He came here later, he likes the sea, he wanted to live here. They've had the shop here for all these years. Started small. Raised the boys here. Sent them to Afrikaans schools, so that they would be part of the community. So they would not be discriminated against unnecessarily, she adds softly. We tried as far as possible to raise them as Afrikaans children, but without forfeiting their Jewish roots.

And are there grandchildren? Magrieta enquires cautiously.

Ezra and his wife have two little boys, says the mother. (Now Magrieta still doesn't know whether Markus is married or not; she doesn't dare ask outright – she doesn't dare show now that she knows nothing about Markus.)

Ezra is the eldest? she asks.

Yes, Markus is their middle child. Perhaps the child who has brought them most worry. He was so highly strung as a child, she adds with a smile.

Magrieta nods. (Highly strung indeed, she thinks, with his unsociability – in spite of his crazy agent talk and irreverent comments.)

The front door opens. Two men enter. The father and one of the brothers, presumably. Magrieta gets to her feet, she is introduced to the father, Samuel, and to Markus' youngest brother, Joshua. They shake hands.

The father has the same reserved manner as Markus, Magrieta can see where Markus' reticence comes from (in Markus it's just been stepped up a hundredfold). With the brother, though, it's quite different: whereas Markus was not inclined to make eye contact, the brother meets her gaze without hesitation. But no self-assured male gaze, and even less an openly erotic or inviting gaze. His gaze is unusually engaging. Overwhelmed by his disarming look, hardly capable of releasing herself from it, she gazes back. The shape of his head is reminiscent of Markus', but his skin is tanned, ruddier than that of his brother. His hair and beard are not as dark as Markus'; cut short, already grizzling in places.

The moment father and son sit down, Magrieta feels painfully uncomfortable. She's an intruder here. She's intensely conscious of the brother's eyes on her – defenceless as two glowing slugs; she can't look at him and she can't look away from him.

Joshua has just returned from Syria and Palestine, the mother says. He was doing volunteer work there in some of the war-torn areas. Joshua nods amiably, says nothing himself, and does not take his eyes off Magrieta for a moment.

She gets up. She's sorry, but she must leave. She's already taken up too much of their time.

No, exclaims the mother, a friend of Markus' is a friend of the family!

She's very sorry, but she has an urgent appointment. (She's lied so much by now, she might as well carry on lying.)

She shakes the father and brother's hands. From the corner of her eye she spots the portraits on the passage wall, among others childhood photos that she would like to look at – surely also of Markus as a child – but she definitely doesn't want to prolong her visit. The mother sees her out. Any time, she says, any time she comes this way again. But Magrieta takes to her heels. In the sky there are small clouds that look like ribs – ribbed clouds like the ribs of a whale.

Her thoughts are in turmoil. She shouldn't have done it. She had no right to be there. She forced herself upon the family. It was underhand to breach Markus' parental home like that under false pretences. She went into their house, abused their hospitality, and saw what was not meant for her eyes to see. She was an opportunist – worse, a voyeur. even. She saw the mother's grief. The vulnerable reserve of the father was not meant for her eyes, the tragedy of his family history was not for her to take note of. And the brother, whose open, compassionate gaze enthralled her so unexpectedly.

She'd got an idea into her head. She'd acted upon it without reflection. Now she can see her folly. She's followed Potsdam far enough. She can see now that, even if she were to follow him even further, try to follow him, as far as the shtetls of his ancestors in Eastern Europe, it would not explain his strange behaviour, because apparently even his mother doesn't know where he is at the moment.

*

Magrieta has lunch at the hotel. She is grateful that the attorney is not there again. The Association of Friends of the Whale, in their wheelchairs, are not present either. No suspect suitcase in the foyer; the meal takes its course smoothly. The food is tasty enough, the sea is calm, the day is fine, the sky is clear, but Magrieta is still upset. She can't shake off the morning's dismay. She feels she's betrayed Markus. If only he hadn't been so strange! If only he'd indicated that the asthmatic agent was somebody he was very close to, that his death had been hard for him. But no, he sits expressionless at his desk with the shirt straining over his shoulders and his high body temperature and he doesn't allow a scrap of it to show. Like David and Jonathan, his mother said. Inseparable.

She decides to walk on the beach before leaving, to the spot where the fish washed up. But first she rests in her room with the curtains closed, to come to her senses.

She is still troubled when she goes for her walk later that afternoon. From the hotel at the far end of the village she walks in the direction of the quay and then all along the beach to more or less the place where she estimates the fish was beached. Naturally no sign of anything here – no drag marks or dark spot where the body lay. A great desolation descends on her. If she stands here and looks at the low mountain gradually sloping up from the town, she thinks she can see more or less the spot where the guesthouse must be where they spent the night. The surroundings are greener than they were then, a good many months ago. She shudders at the memory of her abysmal condition, her pain and nausea in that abysmal little place, with the wind howling around the corners of the house day and night and sweeping unstoppably over all the plain. They would have been so much better off in the hotel. But then she might not have seen the beached whale, and that really was something, even though she was as high as a kite on the quack's toxic medicine. (Do these little places attract every charlatan on earth?)

She sits down on a large rock. High up in the sky a seagull squawks. In her ears the sea rushes. Against her skin she feels the light sea breeze. In her nose is the smell of wet sand, sea, kelp. In the small rock pools at her feet there is a whole secret marine life. In the sea there are whales, now, at this moment. It's the end of September, it's their time. Now, this minute, such a fish might leap from the water ecstatically and fall back, as they are inclined to do, the loudest and most inquisitive of all whale species. That day on the beach in the presence of the dead whale, the silence was like a bell jar that cut her off from all sound. It was just she and the fish and the sensation that she wanted to sink to her knees and shout: I take note! (Of what?! Lord, her head had been so befuddled!)

She is rudely shaken from her reflections when she hears voices. Rolling along on the sand comes a whole phalanx of wheelchairs. The Association of Friends of the Whale is in full cry. Their numbers have swelled considerably beyond the five fellows in the hotel dining room. If she could, she would have kept clear of them – she doesn't feel like this exclusive group now. Enthusiastically talking, singing here and there, with binoculars in one hand and the other hand on some kind of a lever, they come rolling along. (Motorised wheelchairs, otherwise they would have problems moving over the wet sand and wouldn't have their hands free to hold binoculars.)

When the group moves past her, she recognises the five men from last night. They wave cheerily – last night's comments forgotten. They're all wearing the black T-shirts with the logo, and have the same logo on their caps. They greet and call enthusiastically, one by one they roll past her. They are singing a song – presumably to attract the whales. The wheelchair terrorists in the novel were unscrupulous sadists with bulging biceps. They could perform the most incredible feats, up walls and down hills. Killed two poor brothers in the most repulsive way, looking for the tape they thought the brothers had in their possession. Horrific scene. This exuberant group seems harmless. But you never know. A secret organisation, could be a front for something. Who can you trust these days.

There's no point in asking them if they've spotted a whale yet – not if they are an exclusive, or secret, organisation. They'll probably lie, or say they spotted a fish where there was no fish, to put her off the scent. Well, to hell with them.

She stays seated. There go the whale terrorists. She follows them with her eyes until the last one disappears singing around a rock in the distance.

She goes to sit a bit further up against a high dune. It's a windless day. The sun is warm, but not uncomfortably so. She muses, gazing out before her over the sea. She is grateful for the silence. She tries to make sense of her consternation that morning after her visit to Markus' parents. What she's retained of her visit is a feeling of intense shame. She was an impostor there, she deceived those good people. The beneficent warmth eventually makes her drowsy. With her eyes screwed up she gazes half-unseeing over the water.

But when she opens her eyes, by God, high up in the air, *high*, far away, some distance deeper into the sea, but clearly visible, right in front of her unbelieving eyes, a gigantic whale leaps out of the water, graceful and ecstatic, and lands back in the water with an immense splash. And not just once, but again, a second time! The long fluke clearly visible, the hide shimmering in the tremendous rain of spray, the vertical belly grooves unmistakable. A baleen whale.

Magrieta lurches forward onto her knees on the sand, scrambles up, her mouth opens, and a strange sound emanates from her throat. She has to laugh. She has to laugh in disbelief. She has to laugh at her own reaction. She looks around. Is there anyone else about? Is she the only mortal who observed the whale? Nobody, it's the middle of the day and the beach is deserted. For her eyes only that animal leapt from the water, let himself be seen. First the dead fish, and now the live.

She has to think of Jonah. She has to think of Moses and the burning bramble bush. And thrown into the mix other miracles and revelations and annunciations – also the whore who arises from the sea in Revelations she must think of, the one the Uber woman referred to. One minute she's just thinking about a whale, and the next the leviathan reveals himself to her in his full, exuberant glory. His blinding brilliance.

She climbs onto the high rock again, peers over the water, fine-combs the sea with her eyes. She thinks she sees another whale blowing at a distance, maybe more than one. But if there is more than one, the pod is moving away, in the opposite direction to where the wheelchair expedition is heading. (That will teach them to keep their secrets to themselves.)

She stays sitting on the rock. She keeps on scanning the sea, but nothing more. No sign of a whale blowing. Only one singular fish, and two exuberant leaps.

From the corner of her eye she sees someone walking up from the direction of the town.

She recognises him at a distance. It's the brother, Joshua, the man with the extraordinary eyes.

She thinks, this is more than she has strength for at the moment. The dust of her shame has hardly settled, she has barely overcome her feelings of guilt and embarrassment after that morning's visit to the parents, she has just witnessed something out of the ordinary, and here the next challenge comes, walking up – the next obstacle on her path through life.

Nothing to be done about it. She clambers down the rock again and walks up to him hesitantly. When he reaches her and greets her, with his hand, she knows for certain that he's not out for a casual stroll, but that he followed her, or came looking for her. Why did he follow her, is there something he needs to tell her? Something about Markus' whereabouts, perhaps? Could the two of them be in touch without the knowledge of the rest of the family?

For a few moments they stand facing each other without saying anything. Then she points at the sea, and tells him: 'A whale has just leapt from the sea. Twice. A baleen whale. They do it. They fling themselves out of the sea on their backs, out of sheer high spirits.'

The man looks where she's pointing. Then he looks at her with an expression of wonderment. She wonders if he understood properly what she was saying. She hasn't exchanged two words with him, she has no idea how good his Afrikaans still is, if he's just returned from Syria or Palestine where he did volunteer work.

And his eyes! Two lukewarm ocean pools with secret underwater plant life in them.

He smiles at her, but says nothing.

'I was here at the beginning of the year,' she says, 'a dead whale washed up right here. You understand – a whale, dead.'

He nods, but she still doesn't know if he understands what she's saying. She tries to express herself as simply as possible.

'Jonah's fish. Jonah from the Bible.'

He nods and smiles.

'I was,' she places her hand on her heart, the light sea breeze lifts her hair, 'I was so moved by it . . .' She searches for a more comprehensible word. 'It touched my heart so deeply.' She gestures with her hands, makes a movement of her heart welling up.

'You wanted to cry, maybe?' he says. His accent and intonation are a bit strange, the influence of other languages has made itself felt in the Afrikaans sounds, modulated them slightly.

'Yes,' she says, 'I wanted to cry.'

He smiles and nods.

'You came back,' she says. 'How long were you away?'

'I was away for a long time,' he says. 'Almost seventeen years. I did different things. I wasn't home much.'

'You were in war-torn areas. You must have seen a lot. Terrible suffering and hardship.'

'Yes, I saw a lot of suffering and hardship,' he says.

She nods. He smiles.

'Shall we walk back?' she says. They walk in silence for a while.

'Are you staying, or are you going back?' she asks.

'I'm staying for a while. I'll go back later.'

'Have you seen your brother Markus recently?'

'No,' he says, 'too long ago. My mother, she has a hard time. I was away for too long. Markus is away now. I'm waiting to see him. I won't leave before I've seen him.'

Magrieta nods. There doesn't seem to be anything particular about Markus he wants to tell her.

Did he also go to school here, in Vredenburg, like Markus?

Yes, he went to school here with Markus and Ezra, but he left after matric. He didn't want to stay here. The world was too – he shows with his hands – too small. He first went to a kibbutz in Israel for quite a few years.

He suddenly stops. She must please excuse him. His Afrikaans isn't so good any more. His French and Hebrew are better, he says apologetically. He's been out of the country for too long.

She reassures him. There's nothing wrong with his Afrikaans.

They walk on. There's nothing she can ask him about Markus. She doesn't feel like asking him what kind of a man Markus is. She doesn't think he'll know. He's been away for too long. She doesn't know how much contact they had in the years that he was gone. It feels inappropriate, anyway, for her to ask what kind of relationship they have, it's not relevant in a way. This man, newly returned from foreign countries, is so *different* from Markus, she can associate him so little with Markus. He brings with him such a *different* world, he is so open, he looks at her so much as if he is opening himself completely to her. So different, so wholly different from Markus: shy, closed-off, sardonic.

When they reach the hotel, when they stand still at the entrance, when they say goodbye, the man takes Magrieta's two hands in his, first presses her fingers against his lips for a few moments, and then against his heart. Without talking he looks at her. His eyes are without reserve or defence. (With tiny lights in them like phosphorus on water.)

She says goodbye, she turns around and quickly goes up the stairs (the beautiful balustrade cool under her hand) to the first floor. Down the long corridor, her footsteps soft on the thin carpet, the wooden floors springy under her feet.

She sits down on her bed in her room. She hears the sea. A light breeze (fragrant, rich in ozone) lifts the curtain. What is she to make of this, of her visit to Markus' parents, of his brother's last gesture? She has to half-laugh; if she were ever to tell Markus about this: Your brother with the lovely eyes pressed my hands to his lips and then to his heart! She has two conflicting impulses. On the one hand she wants to shake the dust of this fraught place from her feet as quickly as possible; forget about everything that happened here and move on. And on the other hand she would want to stay on in the town for another while – she would in fact rather spend another while in the presence of the brother, bathe in the warmth of his eyes. (Without defence, naked as snails without shells.)

A great turbidity comes over her. She is still ashamed that she presented herself under false pretences to Markus' parents. What was she thinking – that her visit to the town would have no consequences? How fraught this visit has been, like indeed the previous one. First the dead, now the living, fish.

She packs her case. A feeling of loss (a rawness like a wound) grabs her by the scruff of her neck and shakes her till her teeth rattle. She pays her bill. She gets into the car and in the early evening drives back to Stellenbosch.

Sixteen

She has come to new insights, she tells Willem, she has realised her folly. She realises that it was silly to think she could find out anything about Markus Potsdam from his parents. She doesn't know *what* she was thinking. She was so *ashamed* of herself in his parents' house. She agrees with him completely: she has no responsibility towards Markus Potsdam or towards the Bureau. Perhaps she should return on her knees to her former department head at Zoology and ask for her job back. After all, she was an asset to the department.

Willem says: 'Magrieta, don't judge yourself too harshly. You know you are inclined to. And think very carefully before you go back there.'

She tells Willem about the hotel, about the wheelchair association, about the incredible sight of the whale that propelled itself from the water before her eyes. She tells him about Markus' parents and his youngest brother. She says he looks like an empathetic man and he's been doing volunteer service in war-torn areas for a while. She says nothing about his farewell gesture.

She remains troubled: her mind remains turbid, she dawdles before going to bed. Until Willem comes into the room one evening and says: 'Magrieta, calm down. Come here.' And he throws open the sheets invitingly.

She sits down on the bed. He starts caressing her.

'You underestimate me,' she says, half-smiling, half-seriously.

'I don't underestimate you,' he says, 'I think you are delicious, and desirable.'

'You just see me as a sex object,' she says.

'You know that's not true,' he whispers, his mouth in her neck, his hand on her buttocks.

She lies down, her back turned to him. 'You don't take me seriously, you think I have strange whims, you don't respect me.'

'I think you're a loose cannon at times, yes,' he says, now more urgently pressed against her. 'I respect you.'

'You only respect my body,' she says.

'Magrieta . . .' he says.

'What do you think my tragic flaw is?' she asks.

'That you don't want to lie with me more freely,' he whispers in her ear, his hands urgently over her body. 'That you don't let me seduce you every day.'

'I do allow you,' she says, and turns to him.

*

Back at the office, Magrieta says to Isabel: 'Don't laugh. I could see you thought the visit would yield no results, and it didn't. I met his parents and his youngest brother. He's totally different from Markus, you wouldn't say they were brothers.'

'Fuck a buck,' says the girl.

'You can say that again,' says Magrieta. 'But the fact remains, Markus is still missing and that still leaves me in an awkward position. And I'm still worrying about him. I didn't have the courage to tell his mother and them that he's missing. His mother did hint that they're worried about him. He's always been highly strung, and so on. She indicated that he struggles sometimes.'

'I'll say,' Isabel says. 'Struggle seems to be a euphemism in his case.'

'The hotel was nice, at least. We should have stayed there in January instead. We would have had a better time. I wouldn't have fallen. I still think with horror about that dismal guesthouse with the damn wind howling around the corners day and night.'

'Yes, it *was* terrible, actually.'

'And I saw a whale leaping out of the water. Twice. Beautiful!'

'Great!' says Isabel. 'But highly strung or not, that man has pulled a fast one on us.'

'I suppose I should move on,' says Magrieta, dubiously. 'What if he has no intention of ever coming back?'

'Where should you move on to?'

'I don't know,' says Magrieta, 'God knows, I don't know. I suppose I should put all these months at the Bureau behind me and start focusing more seriously on my career again. I suppose I haven't thought hard enough about alternatives.'

'The worms?' the girl says.

'Yes, the worms. I was doing important research. Then something went wrong. Lord knows. Then I went off the rails completely. *Better living through chemistry* was, alas, not to be in my case. And don't laugh again now, because it's my only damn life.'

'I'm not laughing,' says Isabel (but her cheeks are pinker than usual, always a sign).

'Have you *still* not heard from headquarters?'

'No. I don't think they give a flying fuck about what's happening here – or for the fact that we're working with a skeleton staff.'

'Yes. Without a manager's directing hand – and that there's so much damn work that we can barely keep our heads above water.'

*

For days on end Magrieta still thinks with amazement of the strange farewell gesture of Markus' brother with the unusual eyes. So defence-less and compassionate.

*

Magrieta's father was a self-doubting man. He was pessimistic, he was anxious, he was not the kind of father to tell his child: Venture out and

143

conquer the world – especially not his daughter. Careful, he cautioned, careful, there's danger around every corner, careful of the stick, it could poke you in the eye. Careful of the dog, he could bite you. He was tense when he was driving (Magrieta nauseous and carsick in the back from his cigarette smoke), although he liked going on holiday, and liked varied landscapes. Foothills with aloes, thorn trees – those he liked. A loner. Her mother held it against him: He was not the kind of man who should ever have got married, she said. She also maintained that as a child he had been bullied by his brother, just older than him. (Magrieta's Uncle Tobie, with the rasping voice and the hard brush cut). Of his own accord her father would never have said anything like that. About that kind of thing, or about any emotional matter, he never spoke. He believed in corporal punishment. He caned his pupils, Magrieta and her brother.

At the end of her fourteenth year Magrieta started getting restless, disgruntled, dissatisfied with her appearance, thinking she was over-weight. (The start of a serious case of body dysmorphia.) One minute she was still heedless in her own body, the next her body turned against her. At fifteen, in winter, the depression hit her hard. She stopped play-ing sport. She got rid of her snail maze, of her shell and stone collection, of her ant garden. Humboldt's voyages no longer interested her. She read novels, she read fashion magazines, she focused on diets. She started confronting her poor, unsuspecting father; she criticised him, she mocked him. He was a bashful man, not self-assertive, and his only defence against Magrieta was to withdraw himself from her. The more he withdrew, the more viciously she attacked him.

(Why did her mother stay in the shadows? Why did she not step forward and tell her daughter: Enough of this, you don't talk to your father like that? But she was silent. And her father was silent. And her silent brother went his silent way – which he's still doing, after all these years.)

Everybody in the house was silent, and Magrieta, headstrong, rebellious and depressed, defied all discipline and duty. She hated school. School was excessively shit. In her last three years of school she started smoking in secret. She hung out with the wild kids, the fast set – the smokers, the swearers, the drinkers. She taunted the teachers, she was cheeky. She wasn't popular, because she was tall, dark and unpredictable. She kissed boys in their back yard under the fruit trees, but nothing ever came of it. She never had a boyfriend. She wasn't sexy like the other girls. She would diet and then binge. She was in the school's chess team; one winter they went by train to play a chess match at another school. It was cold, for breakfast Magrieta had eaten six pills (diet fad; why did her mother allow it?). She was hungry. The boys in the chess team ate bread on the train. Magrieta watched them resentfully. She was light-headed with hunger. She could hardly concentrate on the chess game. Back home she binged again. In matric she had her eye on the sallow-complexioned cousin of a friend. She was shattered when during an interschool athletics meeting he talked to another girl behind the pavilion. She gave her father hell. She confronted him about religion, about politics. She mocked him about his homosexual brother (a suppressed shame for her father, still of the older generation. Uncle Tobie with the hard black brush cut who as a child had probably tormented her father. Molested him?) She was resentful not only of the boys in her chess team who could eat what they wanted, but also of her brother. She argued with her teachers (her matric biology teacher did not believe in evolution). The children called her a kafferboetie because she vehemently criticised the National Party. She wanted to sleep with the minister, but she had no issue with God. (An attractive man with an ego problem, this minister. Retrospectively.) She didn't want to do her schoolwork. She read novels in the afternoons. She polished off all the novels behind glass in the bookshelf in the passage and in the town library. She wanted to be anywhere but here, in this place, in this classroom, in this school hall, on this miserable Monday morning, in this body.

She liked biology class. She liked things in bottles. She liked drawing the book lungs of the spider and the internal organs of the scorpion. (The sub-oesophageal ganglion, the Malpighian tubules, the pulmonary sacs, the pedipalps, the lateral eyes, the mesenteron.) She liked classifications, she had no problem memorising these things. Her mother signalled her disapproval by withdrawing – by turning away completely from Magrieta, in fact. One evening in matric Magrieta accompanied her friend, her friend's boyfriend and the sallow-faced cousin to a school concert somewhere. They smoked. Afterwards they went to the cousin's house where they drank. Magrieta phoned her mother to say she wasn't coming home. Her mother was violently upset. Magrieta and the cousin spent the night in his bed, without clothes. The cousin didn't even try anything, he'd had too much to drink. When Magrieta got home the next morning, her mother was sitting – in profile – at the kitchen table. She said nothing, she was silent. That was how she showed her disapproval. Magrieta glowed inwardly, she felt fragile, glowing and transparent like a fruit, transported and confused by the previous night's experience of intimacy. She tried lamely to explain that nothing had happened, but her mother said nothing, just kept staring straight ahead.

Magrieta got her last hiding from her father when she was fourteen or fifteen. She had taunted him that evening at the table, incessantly, in the presence of family on a visit. He said nothing, she persisted. Mercilessly. Until eventually he jumped up, grabbed her by the arm (she still tried in vain to hold onto the table leg) and dragged her to her bedroom. There he hit her with a belt. Tearful, furious and humiliated, she stayed in her room, sitting on her bed (in her redecorated room, walls dark grey, bedspread in dark-grey-and-pink abstract motifs). How was she to face the family again? But her favourite uncle, Uncle Chris, her father's youngest brother, the one she liked most of all, knocked on her door a while later with a bit of biltong. Afterwards, for a long time, there were bruises on her arm where her father had grabbed hold of her.

The educational psychologist at school said: medicine, pharmacy or law. Magrieta did not want to be in a profession in which she'd have to help people. She did a BSc with zoology and maths. She studied with a bursary from the Department of Education. It would be easy to pay back the loan, because there was always a demand for science and maths teachers.

For fifteen years she was like somebody walking on the bottom of a river, her hands outstretched unseeing in front of her. She fell in love and the man broke her heart. In the car he recited reams of poems for her (everything – from Homer to Pound, from Blake to Yeats, to Wallace Stevens, John Berryman, Cavafy, Breytenbach). From him she first heard Blake's poem about the worm that flies in the night, in the howling storm, who finds out the rose's bed of crimson joy, and destroys her life with his dark, secret love. They had spectacular arguments. He would rinse his mouth triumphantly with wine before getting into bed with her. Conqueror. Never again could a man wound her like this first one. Never again did anyone make her feel as murderously and as impotently enthralled, or did she thrill in the same way with sexual excitement. She married someone else. Sometimes she felt as if she was standing with a begging bowl in hand. As when you dream you're falling and your heart contracts physically, so her heart often contracted, from early morning to late at night. Sometimes the man ridiculed her, and sometimes he offered her protection. After a few years, she surfaced, spluttering – a child at her breast, a failed marriage, and a lectureship in the Department of Zoology.

Seventeen

It's early October. The trees stand covered in new green leaves, but the first spring rains have not fallen in the Western Cape. The dam levels are still low. The drought has not been broken. In the vineyard the vines produce tiny, hard, bright-green bunches. Potsdam has been missing for almost two months and she's none the wiser as to his whereabouts. If he hadn't left the exhaustive list of instructions for Magrieta – the twelve labours of Hercules – she would have suspected a crime, that perhaps he'd been kidnapped or something. Then it would have been a matter for the police. But he must have suspected that he would be away for a long time, otherwise he wouldn't have set out all the tasks so neatly in advance. What a strange, *ridiculous* situation, she thinks. If it wasn't for Isabel with her cool head, constantly relativising the situation, she doesn't know what she would have done. (Quietly gone off her head?) From Willem she expects no sympathy – he's long not had anything to say about the Bureau or Potsdam.

She told Isabel that she may not have thought hard enough about alternatives, but no alternative had presented itself yet. Going back to the Department of Zoology is unthinkable – she's burned all her boats there, alienated just about all her colleagues, and insulted the head of the department so thoroughly that nobody could blame him for never again wanting to employ her. (She told him among other things that he was an unimaginative and short-sighted petty bourgeois, not a scientist's backside, with no contribution to make in his field. It did not go down well. Behind him stood the departmental secretary, his piece on the side and thick-as-dogshit strumpet of an assistant. Her, too, Magrieta treated to a few unfriendly words, pointed enough to earn her the woman's lifelong enmity as well.)

So if she wants her job back, she'll have to crawl into her former department head's office on her knees, ashes on her head and sackcloth on her body. (The assistant would with relish rest her stiletto heel on Magrieta's head.) She could always submit a letter from the psychiatrist declaring that in that period she had been mentally disturbed owing to the deleterious effects of the wrong medication. (Not that the psychiatrist would be willing to make such an admission.) On the grounds of such a letter the department head would then be prepared to reconsider her position (subject to strict conditions.) Before long she would be reappointed, and would be sitting once again behind her microscope in a white coat, studying the evolution of the nervous and vascular system of the earthworm (the subneural vessels, the seminal vesicles, the median ventral and dorsal blood vessels).

All forgiven, all forgotten, all put behind them, as if she had not been on a path of destruction for weeks (sword in one hand, half-skull in the other; the skull her banner and death her blazon), and furthermore as if she had never seen graffiti behind any door of any toilet, which she later, her head well and truly blown, was tempted to interpret as messages. As if her head had been focused for all those months, and she imperturbably intent on her research.

Improbable scenarios.

After her visit to Markus Potsdam's parents she resolved to let the matter lie. It's out of her hands and she might as well accept that Markus Potsdam will one day turn up again at the Bureau – or not. Time will tell, she hopes. Yet she does, at times, have an urge to invite Bertie Oberholzer for coffee and ask him to tell her everything he remembers about Markus Potsdam and his brothers.

*

It's almost the end of the Bureau's academic year. Mark sheets are submitted. Reports from associates. Applications from students for next year. All of this Magrieta and Isabel must administer – they have their hands full. She gets home late and exhausted every night.

Willem spends a few days in hospital with an old ankle injury that needs surgery. At night Magrieta lies on her own in the conjugal bed; Willem is not here to divert her attention with all manner of seductive suggestions.

She thinks about her life with the earthworm. Darwin has been her hero from an early age. She was still a little girl when her father read her a condensed version of his *Voyage of the Beagle*. She's also going to take a voyage like that one day, she told him. He looked sceptical. Darwin's work on earthworms inspired her own interest. For most people a creepy sort of worm. For her, still now, a fascinating life form. Although the earthworm is a terrestrial animal, it avoided the challenges of a terrestrial life by limiting its activities to a life in damp soil, and by only emerging at night, when there is little evaporation, and by burrowing deep underground during hot, dry weather. Animals well adapted to life on land have a thick, impenetrable hide that limits excessive desiccation, and also prevents respiratory exchange through the hide. For this they need special breathing systems, like lungs. But earthworms breathe in the same way as their aquatic ancestors. That is why they can live for months totally submerged in water, but can't survive when they are dried out.

The earthworm is a double-sided animal – it lives on land, but has not lost the link to its aquatic ancestors. The whale, on the other hand, lives in the sea, but originally roamed the Ordovician plains in the shape of a mid-sized wolf-like land animal.

Her research into the worm took up the major part of her academic life. And then she left the department in disgrace before she could publish the findings of the research project she had been engaged in for the past few years.

*

Magrieta walks the dog on her own for a few afternoons while Willem, out of hospital, can still not put weight on his ankle. First she walks past the school. Litter on the playground. In front of the school building there is a low wall separating two large concrete areas – in the front area a group of boys play with a ball in the late afternoon; the one further back is a neglected netball court, fallen into disuse, with weeds growing in the cracks. A band of energetic white Christian students once did a project with the schoolchildren – they painted the wall and wrote all sorts of uplifting and positive slogans on it: friends, love, play, courage, friendship. On the back of the wall, a Biblical text. The children have in the meantime started drawing graffiti on the wall (words like *frogcock-tongue*, and a very primitive representation of a penis). On one of the windowsills used condoms are visible. On the second storey there is a whole row of broken windows. Past the wall she walks, across the netball court, then up a slight incline, and then she is in the field above the school, and in front of her are the vineyards. Here she still comes across signs of habitation. Sometimes, often under a sparse little tree, there is flattened grass. A liquor bottle. A cigarette packet. A burnt-out fire. Pieces of cloth. Sometimes a garment; why always just *one* shoe? One or more piles of excrement. The underground life. A life under the radar of civilised middle-class life; so totally, *totally* under the radar of white privilege.

(What happened to the woman in her pop-up tent? Magrieta no longer walks that far into the vineyard on her own.)

On one such walk Magrieta comes across a dead hare. A Cape hare. The dog runs around the hare in excited circles, whines softly, runs away and comes back. Curious, Magrieta hunkers down next to the hare. It is lying half on its back, its hind legs spread wide, the front legs together. The neck bent back slightly. The long ears folded back behind the head, their insides visible, with a bluish tinge. The eye is open, but stark, brown, the black pupil enlarged. (So different from the deeply embedded eye of the whale.) The belly fur is white, the rest a light brown, the fur on the head greyer. The hare is not obviously wounded, apart from a slight bloodiness on one of the back paws. Bitten to death by another dog? The light breeze ruffles the fur slightly. When she touches it, the hare is still warm.

It grieves her, a great grief overcomes her at the sight of the dead hare.

Eighteen

Magrieta receives a letter from the Society for the Preservation of Whales, in which they invite her to act as patroness of the society. (She was not aware of the existence of such a body.) Her immediate thought is that the Association of Friends of the Whale (the exuberant black-T-shirt wheelchair-users) passed on her name and address to the society, but those people did not know who she was, unless they got her name and particulars from the hotel management.

Shortly thereafter she receives an invitation to present a paper at a conference in Iceland on the fossil origins of whale-like creatures (Archaeoceti). Why invite *her* to present a paper? In her whole academic career she's never even referred to a whale in a footnote.

The organisers must have obtained her name and particulars from somewhere. From her former department? But after what happened, even the *thought* of her in the departmental corridors, with her overactive synapses and electric hair (Medusa), would prevent them from uttering her name in any context.

Shortly thereafter Agent Buitendach (Dr Ben Buitendach of the natural history museum, where she saw the body of the little Bushman a few months ago) lets her know that they've received an incredible donation from the museum in Cape St Frere. This museum had to close down recently as a result of a lack of government funding. But a huge asset for them – huge in every respect: a whale skeleton! He remembers that she mentioned that she was interested in whales. They've already found a space for it – they'll be able to accommodate it in the large mammal room.

'What kind of whale?' Magrieta asks.

'A baleen whale,' says Ben. '*Megaptera novaeangliae*.'

'A baleen whale!' Magrieta exclaims, amazed.

She asks him please to keep her informed. As soon as the whale has been installed, she wants to come and have a look. She will certainly be able to combine it with a working visit to the town, there are always associates there that she needs to liaise with. Agent Buitendach assures her that he will do so.

She tells Isabel about the two invitations and the whale skeleton. Isabel almost dies laughing (as she laughed about the Association of Friends of the Whale. Especially when she heard they were in wheelchairs). Don't *laugh*, says Magrieta, you're clever, very clever, you need to help me to make sense of these things.

'Look,' she says, 'I like whales, that's true, and last January I had a meaningful whale experience – you were there – that really got my head spinning. When I was in Jameson Bay for a second time, a whale leapt from the water high into the air. Twice. I told you. First the dead and then the living fish. The notices behind the toilet doors before that, too – the cryptic little pictograms – that I didn't take much notice of anyway. Then my daughter sending me WhatsApp photos of a whale skeleton. And now again these three whale things. The whale has been cropping up in my life with disturbing frequency these last few months. Now I'm wondering if there isn't a pattern here – a web of connections perhaps – that I'm not seeing.'

'A web of connections as in a novel?' Isabel asks.

'Yes,' says Magrieta, 'something like that. A code I just can't decipher.'

'Makes a girl think,' says Isabel.

'Look,' says Magrieta, 'with all this whale stuff the element of chance is now becoming a tad extreme, don't you think?'

'I'll have to think about it,' says the girl.

'Is it in fact still chance, or are we talking about some other sinister principle?'

'Stick to chance,' says Isabel, 'you can't go wrong if you stick to chance. Even if it looks left of chance. Beyond chance.'

'But what lies beyond chance?' Magrieta asks anxiously.

'*More* chance,' says Isabel. 'There is probably no end to chance.'

'Chance is infinite, like the universe?'

'Expanding. Chance begets chance.'

'Generates,' says Magrieta. 'Chance generates chance. That I can live with. But the alternative – no.'

The young woman laughs.

*

When Magrieta drops in a few days later on Deneys Swiegers (hoping she won't bump into Bertie), she finds him bitterly upset. So pained she has never seen this man with his usually untroubled countenance. Somebody, she's always thought, who remains untouched by the sphere of messy human emotions and banal everyday concerns.

What's the matter?

The duck has been vandalised.

How?! In what way?!

It looks as if it's been thrown from the table and then hit with something, says Swiegers.

And indeed, on the long table where the duck was always displayed with pride, there is now a cloth draped like a pall over a shape that looks suspiciously amorphous.

Magrieta is shocked. Who would do such a thing? Students? She's read that they recently occupied some of the university buildings. (Perhaps to avenge the uselessness of such a colonial duck. Or purely for the enjoyment of sweeping something from the table that clearly took time and dedication and specialised knowledge and money. Sweep everything from the table that has a trace of colonial initiative, from an excess of undirected ideological passion. She also has to think of the bottles smashed on the school grounds – a sign of an excess of unchannelled testosterone, or of impotent fury, perhaps.)

He doubts it. He has a strong suspicion who did it, but he dare not say it out loud before he has proof.

It can be only one person. 'Bertie?' she says.

He nods.

'But why?' Although she knows. Has Bertie not sat in her office lamenting Swiegers' treatment of him? But to go to such an extreme – *that* she wouldn't have expected of Bertie. That's what you get, she thinks, when two people can't sort out a quarrel over a duck!

'Where is he now?'

'He would have gone on leave the day before yesterday. I found the duck yesterday.'

'What now?'

'Start from scratch. Repairing the damage will take *months* of work,' he says, 'the time and money are almost incalculable.' She thinks she sees something like tears welling up in his eyes. She is startled by his shattered expression – so different from his normal equable gaze. For the first time – and with quite a shock – Swiegers suddenly reminds Magrieta of someone against whom she still bears a grudge, after all these years. A colleague. The same open, boyish face. Odd that she should only now make the association. Yes, she thinks, here he sits now with his pained countenance, when he probably has a solid share in the whole mess.

'Are you going to confront him about it?' she asks.

'Not until I'm quite sure it was him.'

'And if it is, would the university take disciplinary steps against him, dismiss him?'

Swiegers shrugs. He doesn't know. It could probably be seen as damage to university property.

Now is obviously not the time to discuss Bureau business or anything else with Deneys Swiegers. She'd hoped to sound him out on the subject of chance, apropos of her conversation with Isabel. Quite perturbed, she leaves. She's sorry for him, sorry about the heavy damage to the duck, but she's sorry for Bertie too – if it was him – that his feelings drove him to such an extreme act.

She dreams that night that Markus Potsdam is lying in shallow water with his eyes open. She lies down next to him. What does the dream mean? she wonders. Is Potsdam dead, for her to dream of him with these staring, open eyes?

*

When she gets to the office the next morning, Isabel comes to meet her with big eyes and flushed cheeks.

'Fuck a buck,' she says. 'Potsdam is back. He's sitting in his office, at his computer, as if he hasn't been gone for a single day!'

Magrieta can't believe it.

She knocks gently at his door before entering. Her heart is beating wildly. He gets to his feet clumsily when she enters. God knows, he's at his computer, in the same kind of shirt he always wears – indeed as if he's never been away.

'Hello, Markus,' she says, 'what a pleasant surprise to have *you* back again.' It wasn't her intention to sound so snide.

'Hello, Magrieta,' he says.

He says nothing more. Waits for her to say something.

'You've been away for quite some time.'

He nods.

'You didn't say how long you'd be away for.'

'No,' he says, 'I didn't.'

'Did it occur to you that we might be worried?!' She doesn't want to sound accusatory, but can't help herself.

'It must have been inconvenient for the two of you,' he says.

'Inconvenient!?' she exclaims. 'It was more than that!' Now that she's started she can't stop. 'Did you even think that it could have jeopardised our own plans? Isabel and I could only just cope with all the work. But that's still okay' – she makes a dismissive gesture with her hand – 'we managed after a fashion – what's worse is how worried I was!'

He says nothing. Looks down in front of him.

'Isabel reckoned you'd walked into the sea,' she says.

He looks up in surprise. 'Did she?'

'Yes, she did. It's a hunch she had.'

He nods slowly.

'May I ask where you were?' she asks, more accommodatingly.

'Yes, Magrieta, you may,' he says. 'I had myself committed to an institution six weeks ago. A psychiatric institution. For depression. Isabel is an observant woman. I *did* consider walking into the sea. Among other things.'

She feels her cheeks reddening. The carpet pulled out from under her feet. She didn't expect this.

'Why didn't you say something, Markus? I don't understand it! You could have said you were depressed, you wanted to go away for a while. Then we could have made other plans!'

He stares straight ahead, nods slowly.

'What did you *think*, that it's a disgrace, being depressed?' she asks. 'Did you have some ridiculous notion that one should suffer in solitude?!'

His gaze is fixed.

'And your cousin who died! Terrible! Why didn't you tell me? I'm still ashamed of myself that I referred to him as the asthmatic agent. And you didn't correct me. Really, Markus, you could have said something. You could have given some kind of indication of your state of mind.'

Potsdam looks up. Looks straight at her. 'I appreciate your concern, Magrieta,' he says. 'I sincerely appreciate it. And I realise you and Isabel must have had your hands full. I was aware of it all the time, all too aware. It didn't help. I can never thank the two of you enough. Or reward you adequately.'

'That's not necessary either, Markus. It's over and done with now. If only I could understand what it was about, what was happening in your head. I heard you crying one evening in your office. I should have confronted you, instead of clearing out so damn politely.'

He looks down again, in front of him.

'I suppose I should congratulate you,' says Magrieta, 'that you did manage to have yourself admitted – before you did something irresponsible.'

'Like walking into the sea,' says Markus, glancing up briefly.

'Yes, like walking into the sea. Well,' she says, 'did it help?'

'We'll have to see,' he says. 'It probably did. A bit.'

'I'm sorry, Markus,' she says. 'I'm really sorry to hear it.'

'Thank you,' he says.

She gets up, but sits down again. 'What did you *think*, Markus?' she says. 'That your depression would be a burden to us? Instead of which you burdened us with your silence. You know, don't you, that I went to visit your parents to try to find out where you were? I met your mother and father and Joshua. Your mother told me about your cousin. I'm so sorry about that, Markus. I was so ashamed afterwards. I felt like an impostor in your parents' home.'

'It's not necessary to be ashamed, Magrieta. I'm the one who should be ashamed.'

'I was a fool all the same,' she says.

'Who do you think was the fool here, Magrieta?' he asks. 'And who is, still?'

'How do you mean?'

'It was unforgivably short-sighted of me to think I could run this place in the first place.'

'Well . . .' she says.

'Do you think I wasn't aware that the two of you were running the Bureau practically on your own?'

'Well . . .' says Magrieta.

Markus exhales deeply, turns his head away. His desk is still clear.

His office is still empty. He's got thin. His wrists look vulnerable. He keeps his head turned away, he looks out of the window. It's the first time she sees him in profile.

'Do you think I would have spoken about it if I could? When you feel the way I felt, it's not interesting,' he says softly, 'not to yourself, not to others.'

'Well . . .' says Magrieta.

'You feel dead and your deadness is not interesting.'

He is silent for a while. Still gazes out of the window.

'You feel as if you're dead to yourself and to others. You don't get past it – past your own deadness.'

His words frighten her.

He is silent for a while again. Then he suddenly turns to her, faces her squarely, and says matter-of-factly, as if discussing a Bureau matter: 'There wasn't a single cell in my body that wasn't permeated. Every one of my cells was permeated with the rot of futility. It's not the kind of feeling you can or want to communicate to others. It's just something you want to put an end to.'

Shocked, she says nothing.

'I didn't want to burden my parents with my condition. They've had a hard enough time. But all I could think of,' he says 'was ending it all.'

She's sitting here before this uncommunicative, taciturn man and for the first time he's talking about himself. It's enough to make her teeth chatter.

'I tried,' he said. 'I went to stay in a friend's house at the sea. My attempt did not succeed. I'll spare you the humiliating details. That's when I had myself admitted.'

'I hope things will be better from now on,' she says. It sounds so feeble.

Markus is still facing her squarely: 'We'll have to see,' he says.

'And I'm sorry about my ridiculous SMSs,' she says, getting up. 'I'm so ashamed that I pestered you with those as well!'

He smiles a little, shakes his head, as if wanting to reassure her, but says nothing.

Isabel is waiting with flushed cheeks in her office. Her own cheeks burn with discomposure.

'You were right,' says Magrieta, 'he *did* consider walking into the sea, in a manner of speaking. He tried to do himself in, but his attempt clearly failed.'

'What now?' asks the girl.

Magrieta shrugs. 'Now nothing. I have no choice. I carry on with what needs to be done. Now that I know what Potsdam's situation was, it puts things in a different perspective.'

'The wisdom of hindsight.'

'No wisdom here. But let's talk about something else. I need to process the shock of Potsdam's return.'

'Yes,' says the girl. 'It's hectic. I got the fright of my fucking life when I saw him sitting in his office this morning. Is he okay now?'

'I don't know. We'll have to see. The poor man.'

'Fuck a buck.'

'But I can't *believe* it,' says Magrieta, 'all the weeks that he was away, when I was so worried . . .'

'And we just about worked our butts off.'

'Yes. And one fine day it's all just over. There he sits again. As if he never left.'

'At least we're left with the wisdom of hindsight,' the girl says.

'Don't mock. I still know nothing. That's the worst. Apart from the fact that he was so depressed that he wanted to take his own life, I still know nothing about him.'

'Yes, I suppose that's so,' says Isabel.

'*Nothing*,' says Magrieta, 'absolutely *nothing*. All that I know is that it was the longest, most personal conversation I've ever had with him. I suppose I should be grateful that it could happen at all.'

'Yes,' says the girl, 'I suppose that's something.'

'But it does make my situation even more difficult, in a way.'

'How come?'

'I can't just up and leave now.'

'Why not? You can abandon the sinking ship without qualms now.'

'No, not before I know that he's totally okay!'

'I think,' says the girl, 'as soon as I've left one of these days, the very best option will be for you *and* Potsdam to find something else and lock the Bureau door behind you once and for all. Throw away the key. Headquarters won't even notice. I don't know about him, but you can go back to looking after your worms.'

'For God's sake, Isabel,' says Magrieta, 'just don't remind me now, please, that you have to leave one of these days. It's bloody well more than I can cope with today.'

Nineteen

Magrieta's great-grandfather was born in 1882, the year that Élie (Ilya Ilyich) Metchnikoff, the Russian-born zoologist, started developing his theory of cellular immunity. Of this theory her great-grandfather remained ignorant. His eldest son was born in 1905, the year Albert Einstein sorted out space and time. Of this her great-grandfather knew as little as he did about Metchnikoff's theory; it was three years after the end of the Anglo-Boer War, he was a member of the police force in Barberton, and they had their hands full with rounding up stock thieves and other miscreants. In 1907 his second son was born and in 1909 his third son, Magrieta's grandfather, the year in which the Burgess Shale was discovered. Charles Doolittle Walcott, an American palaeontologist, by chance, on 31 August, while crossing from Mount Field to Wapta Mountain, noticed fossils in a block of scree and immediately recognised their importance. In the course of the next eight years he excavated about 70 000 specimens, which he sent to the Smithsonian Institution in Washington. The full extent of the find, however, was largely revealed by the British palaeontologist Harry Whittington, his research students and Canadian palaeontologists. By the time Magrieta's grandfather had grown into his senses, the Cape Rebellion of 1914 and the First World War had both run their course. (Magrieta's great-grandmother would have eight more children after the grandfather's birth.) Magrieta's father, her grandfather's second eldest son, was born in 1932, seven years before the beginning of the Second World War. He had five more siblings; his youngest sister, Aunt Hettie, was born in 1945, at the end of the war, but it was her Uncle Christiaan, the second youngest, born in 1942, to whom Magrieta was very attached. Magrieta was born in 1968, the year in which the American theoretical physicist Murray Gell-Mann discovered that the so-called fundamental particles – the neutrons, protons, anti-neutrons, anti-protons, pions, kaons, lambdas and sigmas – consist of yet simpler particles, which he named quarks.

*

In matric, when Magrieta was still displaying antisocial behaviour (she didn't want to take part in activities, she didn't want to go to school, she was rebellious and confrontational in class, she was uncommunicative at home, she was clearly very unhappy), the family doctor told her mother that Magrieta should see a therapist. Once a week her father took her to the practice, quite a distance from their home. (Her mother could not drive yet.) In the car on the way there they did not exchange a single word, and in the car on the way back they did not exchange a single word. They had for some time lacked any basis on which to communicate. (Her father's generation didn't see therapy as something normal or desirable; for him, there was a stigma attached to it.) Magrieta sat next to her father in the passenger seat, angry and ashamed. These car trips were almost more than she could endure – here, week after week, in this car, in this body, with her father on this agonising trip. (In retrospect, Magrieta thinks the therapy itself didn't amount to much.)

*

In her twenties Magrieta had to have the intra-uterine contraceptive she was using removed because it made her bleed too much. It would be done in the doctor's consulting rooms. Her father took her there. He didn't know why she was going to see the doctor, and he didn't ask. The removal did not go as smoothly as it should have. Afterwards she had severe pain and bled copiously. What was her father to think of the fact that there was nothing wrong with her when he dropped her (he waited for her in the car), but that she returned to the car nauseous and white with pain? He asked no questions, she offered no explanation. If he suspected something, he said nothing. What was there to say in any case? There was no way she could explain to him why she was in pain. The word menstruation wasn't even used in his presence. (The humiliating fact was tactfully never mentioned.)

She bled so heavily that once, when returning from town by bus, she had a large bloodstain on the back of her skirt. In her youth and young adulthood she was ashamed of the blood and of her body. She was so often ashamed, angry and filled with longing. An indeterminate, wistful, fruitless longing.

Twenty

Bertie Oberholzer turns up outside Magrieta's door at the Bureau. She invites him in.

When he's seated, he keeps his eyes cast down, avoids her glance. She waits for him to speak.

Had she heard that Swiegers' duck had been damaged?

Yes, she had, and Swiegers is enormously upset.

Bertie nods, he looks miserable. Yes, he says, Swiegers is upset.

She decides to ask him straight out: 'Bertie, do you know something, did you have anything to do with this?'

No, he did not. But he shuffles uncomfortably in his chair and still avoids her eyes.

'Do you know anything about it?'

'Yes.'

'What do you know?'

'It was a student. At least, I *suspect* it was a student.'

'What makes you suspect that?'

'There is somebody who came to complain to me. More than once. Swiegers often treats the students very bluntly.'

'So?'

'So the student said he'd had enough. He was fed up. He and other students. Swiegers is a racist as well. He looks down on black students.'

'And?'

'He was going to do something.'

'Did he say what he was planning to do?'

'No.'

'Bertie, look at me, did he say what he was planning to do?'

Bertie looks up at her beseechingly. 'No, he didn't say.'

'Bertie,' says Magrieta, 'did you encourage the student in any way to damage the duck?'

Bertie looks up shocked, close to tears. How could she say a thing like that? How could she even *think* it? He is opposed to the duck, that he won't deny. He's explained to Magrieta why. But he swears he would never go as far as being complicit in vandalising it. The student was angry. Very angry. Other students as well. They all complain that Swiegers is stingy with marks. He's too strict. He thinks black students are inferior.

'Do you think it's true, do you think Swiegers looks down on black students?'

'I don't know,' says Bertie, 'but I believe the student, he wouldn't lie.'

Is the man lying through his teeth here, Magrieta wonders, because he's just too het up – his cheeks are just too red, and his story just *too* plausible.

Magrieta looks up, over the man's head to the mountains far in the background. It's dry. It won't rain. Her garden is withering with the water restrictions. She is tired. She has no desire to deal with this fellow this morning. She feels desperately sorry for Swiegers about the duck, he didn't deserve it. She doesn't even want to *think* of the extent of the loss in terms of time and funding. Must Bertie come to burden her with his story now?

'Have you discussed your suspicions with Swiegers?' she asks.

'No,' he moans, 'I haven't.'

'Are you planning to do so?'

He doesn't know. He thinks Swiegers should know, but he also doesn't want to cast suspicion on the student. The student took him into his confidence.

'If I were you, Bertie,' she says, 'I'd go and talk to Swiegers as soon as possible.'

When she gets up to accompany him to the door, Magrieta says, 'By the way, Markus Potsdam is back. Do you want to say hello, maybe?'

But Bertie just about staggers back. 'No, please, not today, another time, maybe!' And he rushes out.

*

After her conversation with Markus regarding his depression they don't discuss it again. But when she goes into his office a few days later, he doesn't look well. It doesn't look like he's thriving. He is thin. His face is pale. There's something restless about his movements, and he's avoiding eye contact again.

'Are you okay, Markus?' she asks.

'Yes,' he says. Feeble smile.

'Are you really okay, or are you just treading water?' (She would not have asked such a direct question before, but she reckons that with their last conversation they crossed a line.)

'I'm taking my medication,' he says.

'But is it helping?' she asks.

He shrugs. The doctor says he must be patient. It's still too early to tell whether it's the right medicine.

Sounds familiar, she thinks. 'If there's anything I can do,' she says, 'please let me know. Take it easy.' Lord, she thinks, that sounds so feeble.

He nods.

'I told you, didn't I, that I met your brother?' she says.

'I heard.' (So he's resumed contact with his family.)

'Has he left again?' she asks.

'He's leaving in a week or so.'

'Where to?'

'Palestine. Syria. It's not always possible to keep track.'

'That's brave of him. He struck me as an exceptional person. Lots of empathy with others.'

Markus nods. He looks away. She can't read his expression.

She wants to ask him if he has a support network – a wife or a husband or a loved one or someone close to him, but Markus is already peering at his computer, always a sign that the conversation is over. She must be careful with the personal questions, she thinks. In their last conversation they already covered more ground than in all the preceding months.

She hesitates, but says nevertheless: 'One more thing.'

He looks up.

'Why did I have to meet your cousin, Markus?'

He looks down. Is silent for a moment. Then looks up. She's startled at his bereft look. She doesn't want to see him like that – so bereft and grief-stricken. Then rather his usual businesslike façade.

'There was no reason for you to meet him. He would have dropped in on my parents that weekend and I was to meet him there. He was on his way to Namibia. I didn't feel up to seeing either my parents or him. I was in a very bad way. I didn't want the people closest to me to see me in that state. I hoped to be able to think up something closer to the time . . . well . . .'

'Perhaps a message I had to deliver on your behalf?' she asks.

'Yes. A message, maybe. Or something.' He shrugs half-indifferently.

'Oh dear,' she says.

'Then he died unexpectedly. He was an asthma sufferer, but it was completely unexpected. So then I tried for the first time to end it all. When I got the news. It didn't work, like the second time. Laughable, actually.'

'I'm so sorry, Markus,' she says.

'Yes,' he says, ' we were close.'

'Like David and Jonathan, your mother said.'

'Yes.'

'Markus, please,' she says, 'say when things start going badly again. Don't wait until it's unbearable.'

'No,' he says, 'no.' But to her mind he says it without conviction.

When she leaves the office, a distressing phrase occurs to her: Third time lucky.

'Potsdam doesn't look good to me,' she tells Isabel. 'I'm now *really* worried about him. I don't know if he has a support network. It doesn't look as if his pills have kicked in. In no time he'll be back in the institution. Or worse.'

'Fuck a buck,' says the girl.

'You can say that again,' says Magrieta. 'Fucking twice and thrice a fucking buck.'

*

She says to Willem: Do you think I've changed in the past few months, since starting to work at the Bureau? Do you think I'm more obsessive than usual?

Willem just laughs. This kind of talk doesn't interest him. As long as she's not conspicuously crabby, and doesn't complicate things unnecessarily, and is receptive to him, he has no truck with speculations of this kind. All he says is: Magrieta, I've said it so many times, you have to get out of that place. You're wasting your abilities. It wouldn't surprise me if you went off the deep end completely there. (They both forbear to mention that she went off the deep end when she was sitting in a white coat, behind a microscope, in a laboratory, where she should have felt most in her element.)

Willem is solidly built, his blond hair is starting to grizzle in places. He has light-blue eyes, which betray his Northern European roots (Viking ancestors); sometimes she can't stop staring at his eyes – so *eye-like*, so clearly an organ of sight. It seems to her that the blue of his eyes is getting a bit weathered nowadays, as if the iris is losing its hard blue glitter. On the face of it such a level-headed man, but at the same time so vulnerable, with emotions running so deep underground.

After work, before supper, she and Willem sometimes lie together on their bed for a while. He usually lies behind, she in front. In summer they lie in the small, cool guest room on the single bed. He talks about what interests him – the state of the economy, cricket, business transactions, his computer problems, problems at work. She doesn't really talk herself, but she doesn't really listen either. Her previous lovers were right, she's often inattentive. Her first husband said she might as well have been deaf and dumb and blind, so little did she listen to him, so little did she *see* him; she didn't pay attention to what was *important*. (She tried to mend her foolish ways, but apparently didn't succeed.) What, then, was her gaze focused on, all those years? On the ventral and dorsal grooves of the earthworm? On millions of years of invertebrate evolution? On her child, about whom she always worried so needlessly? (The woman in the vineyard maintained that motherhood is a terrible fate, for the mother but especially for the child, who suffers irreparable damage from it.) If she thinks back on her inner life of all those years, it seems as if her head had always been like an uninhabited ant hill – full of empty loops and bends.

But with Willem's hand on her buttocks, on her back, in her hair, when they're lying together like that, she comes to a halt, her mind a void. BLISS. This is the closest she comes to contentment, she thinks. She's grateful that Willem doesn't tell her his dreams. She would find it difficult to listen to them. Her first husband regularly told her his dreams, it alienated her from him, these strange dream narratives that he expected her to listen to, and when her attention wandered, he'd rebuke her.

*

Bertie Oberholzer phones her one evening quite late – shortly after so vehemently denying his own part in the vandalising of Swiegers' duck. (Where did he get her telephone number?)

Can he please see her immediately?

It's late, Bertie, she says, can it wait till tomorrow?

No, it can't. It can't, it's a matter of life and death! (She can tell from his voice that he's intensely upset.)

A matter of life and death, she thinks, well, well, what can it be? Must have something to do with the duck. But life and death?!

Where is he, she wants to know, does he know where she lives?

Oh yes, he knows. He's in the car, outside her house.

Willem is annoyed, why do people bother her at home in the evening? It will probably not take long, she assures him. She'll get the fellow out of here as soon as possible.

Bertie looks dreadful and he smells of smoke and drink – not wine, spirits. He's wearing odd clothes. Not his usual check shirt, shorts and walking boots. Tonight he's wearing a strange, flamboyantly striped shirt (*very* ugly, synthetic cloth), jeans (terrible cut) and slip-slops. Magrieta invites him in and immediately takes him to the kitchen.

Can she make him some coffee?

Yes, please.

He looks pale in spite of his ruddy complexion, very pale. His skin looks ice cold; his hair is wet with perspiration, and unkempt.

He sits down on one of the high stools and immediately rests his head on his arms on the counter.

She puts the coffee down in front of him.

'Is something the matter, Bertie?' she asks.

Stupid question, of course something's the matter, he said himself it's a matter of life and death.

'My life is over, it's tickets for me and my career.' His tongue is thick and his eyes seem out of focus. It looks as if he's blinking them more slowly than usual.

It must be the duck.

'Is it in connection with the duck?' she asks, wearily. She glances at the wall clock. It's half past ten. She's tired.

'Yes,' he says.

She waits. He adds three spoons of sugar to his coffee and takes a large gulp.

'I fucked everything up,' he says. It's the first time she's heard him swear.

'How come, Bertie?'

'It was me,' he says, 'I was the one who attacked Swiegers' duck.'

'Oh hell, Bertie!' she says. (Attacked, she thinks, as if the duck were a person.)

'I had such a desire,' he says, 'to smash that damn duck to smithereens!'

He takes another gulp of coffee. Stares straight ahead as if contemplating the scene of the crime and the violated duck in front of him.

'Fuck,' he says, '*fuck* that fucking duck!'

Magrieta suddenly has an irresistible urge to laugh. Flustered, she wants to laugh because it's funny, but also because it's dreadful. Now she knows what Isabel must feel like when she has to suppress a fit of laughter.

Bertie bangs his fist on the granite top. 'Why did I ever set foot in that building?' (Every word is punctuated with a blow of his fist.) 'I *knew* it wouldn't work out! I *knew* I should avoid Deneys at all costs! I *knew* he was bad news! Bad, bad, bad news!'

Magrieta takes a sip of her tea. It's going to be a long night, she can see. She hopes Willem doesn't get too impatient.

'Because he didn't give you recognition for the work you did?'

'No,' says Bertie, 'that too, but not only that.'

He takes a sip of coffee. Hardly aware of what he's drinking. Gazing ahead of him. The colour seems to be seeping back into his cheeks.

'That duck is *reprehensible*,' he says suddenly with renewed passion. 'It's a *reprehensible* project. And Swiegers is a *reprehensible* human being! He's low, he's mean, he's manipulative, he's an emotional exploiter!'

Magrieta remembers again the sudden connection she made with her former colleague when she last saw Deneys Swiegers, the day the damaged (deceased) duck lay behind them on one of the tables in the laboratory under a cloth – an association she had not had before with Swiegers. She'd not thought about it again, because shortly thereafter Markus Potsdam had returned, and then she'd had to deal with *that* development.

'Bertie,' Magrieta asks, 'what do you *actually* have against Swiegers?'

'I can't say,' says Bertie, and he leans forward again with his head on his arms, sobbing.

He lifts his head, and through his tears he says: 'He abused me! He toyed with my emotions! He knew I would do *anything* for him! Anything!'

'Oh, good heavens, Bertie,' says Magrieta, feebly, as she starts to suspect what goes where in this intrigue.

'At first,' says Bertie, 'I thought I would give the laboratory key to the student. Then he could do what he wanted in the laboratory. If he wants to fuck the duck up in the process, fine. Then I thought I couldn't do it to the student, it's cowardly of me to endanger *his* career. And besides . . .'

But he interrupts himself suddenly, looks up, and fixes his tearful gaze on something behind Magrieta, a small painting on one wall of the kitchen. It's a little oil of the wreck of the *Medusa*, a ship that ran aground on the West Coast in the nineteenth century. It's painted in a semi-naïve style; the ship, capsized, is depicted from a high vantage point, with a lot of activity on the beach in the foreground. Tiny clusters of people, it looks as if there's even a military camp pitched there, and, a short distance away, huts probably belonging to the Khoi. He gazes at it long and attentively, as if he has suddenly forgotten everything that brought him to this point, in this kitchen: everything that preceded the point where he could no longer bear it and wanted to demolish the duck.

'It's very beautiful,' he says. Magrieta nods. She loves it herself, she says. He nods distractedly. 'In any case, I wanted to fuck that thing up myself,' he suddenly continues vehemently. 'I didn't want to give any-one else the pleasure.' He goes quiet, again focusing his gaze on the little painting. 'But I couldn't. I just couldn't bring myself to do it. I thought of how much the duck meant to Swiegers, and how badly he'd take it. The reason why I *wanted* to do it was also the reason why I *couldn't* do it.'

Willem peers around the corner, behind Bertie's back. Magrieta sig-nals with her eyes it's okay.

'So I closed my eyes and swept the duck off the table. And when it hit the ground I gave it an almighty kick. And then another.'

'Well, that's a bit better, Bertie,' says Magrieta, because she doesn't know what else to say, 'than smashing it to smithereens.'

'Oh well,' he says, 'Deneys knows it's me. It doesn't really matter any-more. The damage has been done. Now he'll just despise me even more. And rightly so. It was a *despicable* act.'

'Don't judge yourself so harshly, Bertie,' says Magrieta, but he doesn't even hear her, he just stares in front of him, unseeing, tearful. 'Perhaps you should talk to Deneys anyway,' she says.

'*Talk?*' he says, '*talk* to him? Talk to someone who's already hardened his heart against you?'

He gazes bleakly into the middle distance.

'If he even *has* a heart,' he adds. 'That fucking *duck* has a softer heart than Deneys.'

'I'm sorry, Bertie, I didn't realise it was that bad.' (Of heartlessness she would never have suspected Deneys – not with his open face and friendly manner.)

'It's even worse,' he says.

Magrieta sits, she doesn't know what to say to him. She's always found him a bit ridiculous, but now he seems heroic to her in his misery.

'Can I make you some more coffee?' she asks.

'No, no thanks,' he says, and gets to his feet abruptly. 'I must go. I'm grateful that I could talk to you, Magrieta.'

'It's a pleasure, Bertie.'

It's quarter to twelve. He seems steadier on his feet when she sees him off, less woozy. She remains standing at the door until he gets into his car and drives away, with who knows what plans and resolutions in his distressed head.

'What was *that* about?' Willem asks when she gets into bed.

'A crime of passion,' she says.

'Do you feel like committing a crime of passion with me?' he asks, his mouth in her neck.

That may be the only thing that will calm her down, she says. (That will distract her, she thinks, from Deneys Swiegers, from Bertie Oberholzer, from the deflowered mechanical duck, and from the troubling memory of her erstwhile colleague. Someone she'd regarded as a friend, but who stole her research and, on top of that, blackened her name among his new colleagues when he went North.)

*

The next morning Magrieta tells Isabel about Bertie Oberholzer's visit to her the night before. It's odd, she says, whether Bertie's accusations are founded or unfounded, she'll never be able to look at Deneys Swiegers in the same way. (What she doesn't say is that she'll never be able to think of him as altogether honourable again.) Just as she'll never be able to look at Markus Potsdam in the same way, she says, now that she knows what happened to him.

And from now on, Magrieta thinks, Markus Potsdam will always be the middle son of the worried mother, the cousin of the dead agent, to whom he was as close as David to Jonathan, and the brother of the man with the soft, compassionate gaze. The man who took her hands in his, brought them to his lips and then pressed them to his heart, and on whom she there and then could have hung her heart, the day they parted in front of the hotel, before she ran up the stairs to her room.

When for a moment she strongly considered turning back and going after him. She often wonders about that – what would have happened if she'd done it.

Twenty-one

Just to the left of the school entrance there's a shipping container in which a guard presumably used to sit. Now it's empty, because the school gate has long since been stolen (yanked off its hinges). The children draw graffiti on it – mainly names, but here and there also a few images. There is a large representation of a girl's face that looks like a child's drawing. With an empty speech bubble emerging from her mouth, arms that end in something like square sleeves, and a torso consisting only of two buttocks – no legs. Under the buttocks is the schematic representation of a penis and two testicles.

'It looks like three cactus leaves,' says Willem, 'three cactus leaves of the same size meeting in the middle.'

Magrieta laughs, yes, indeed. The hairs on the testicles look like the spikes on these cactus leaves – four spikes on the one and five on the other. A legless, handless, breastless, smiling girl with a disembodied penis ready to penetrate her.

A second drawing is even more schematic. Torsoless buttocks are penetrated by an almost identical shape intended to depict a penis and testicles. The penetrated shape could be a vagina or an anus; no indication whether it's a front or a back view. Below, next to two scratched-out names is written: IS POESES.

A heart-shaped buttock shape is penetrated by a disembodied penis and testicles, coloured red. Willem says the red shape could just as well be read as excrement – shit, but Magrieta thinks at first that it represents a little pool of menstrual blood.

Next to a very small, schematic representation of a penis and scrotum somebody has written his name in conspicuously large, fancy graffiti calligraphy: DUWAYNE. Next to a large, exceptionally long, thin penis, with very small testicles underneath, someone has written: *a pussy prick.*

But the most engaging little drawing, tiny, is in one lower corner of the container. It looks like a space rocket (Willem remarks) ascending while belching out a cloud of flame. The lower part of the rocket represents the lower part of the body, the stabilising tail fins are the two legs. (Magrieta laughs at Willem's description.) The exhaust gases are then the vertical penis shaft, and the billowing smoke cloud is the outline of the scrotum.

In between the drawings are names, mainly girls' names. Some names have been scratched out. Willem says he wonders what these graffiti mean to the boys and girls who walk past every day or stand here and talk.

After looking at these for a while, Magrieta and Willem walk on, past the wall (with more graffiti), over the neglected concrete netball court, up a small incline – on the right a piece of veld with long grass and a few wattle trees, or Port Jacksons. People chop wood here, and do their business while they're at it, because there is often a suspect smell hanging in the air. Across a dirt road – everywhere among the vineyards are dirt roads for tractors and the trucks loading the grapes – and then they are in the vineyard. The bunches of grapes are still small and green, they will start to swell later.

When they walk past a few smallish trees on the left, Magrieta gets a fright, she hadn't seen the man! He's sitting against the low bank, staring straight ahead. They greet him, but he doesn't look around. He sits with his back half-turned to them, in semi-profile. For a moment Magrieta isn't sure if he's pulled his pants down and is defecating, but then she sees that's not the case. He's sitting motionless, a hard, dark profile. It's in this vicinity that the flattened grass, empty bottles, discarded garments, empty cigarette packets indicate human habitation. This must be one of the places where the little nomadic bands hang out (sojourn, linger, camp out), those who move under the radar, those who would certainly have come across the woman here in the vineyard. It must be one of those she may have recognised as a fellow pilgrim.

*

Agent Buitendach reports that he and Barry Cilliers will be taking delivery of the whale skeleton in a week's time. They want to disassemble it themselves, because it's a big job, it's going to take them quite a while. They're renting a special truck in which they'll transport it to Albany West. There it will have to be carefully reassembled. A big job, but they are very excited. A wonderful donation, he says again. She must come and have a look as soon as it's been installed. The university is releasing funds for the project. They are grateful, these days there's not that much money for this kind of project. Magrieta promises, she'll come and have a look, she's dead keen to see the skeleton. And it's a big one, Agent Buitendach adds.

She's holding thumbs, says Magrieta, she hopes all goes well with the transport and installation.

*

One afternoon when Willem is working late, Magrieta decides, for the first time in a long while, to walk the route again to the part of the vineyards where she came across the woman.

She gets a fright when at a distance she sees somebody sitting on the rock where the woman used to sit. (The last time with a little bunch of sweet, warm grapes in her hand.) The sun is shining in her eyes, she can't see that well. Her first thought is: It's the woman, she's survived, she actually survived all those months! But when she gets closer, she sees it's not the woman. It's a young man, sitting placidly on the rock with his legs crossed, smoking. The sun behind him illuminates his head of hair like a halo.

When he notices her, he leaps to his feet (he must also have got a fright), puts out his hand and introduces himself as Ashley Fondant. Very definitely not one of the people she usually comes across here, mainly farm workers. He's wearing interesting loose pants, a funky little shirt that reaches to just above his waist and reveals his trim, sexy brown tummy, and his hair has been fashionably cut – clean-shaven on the sides, with a dense, curly mop on top of his head.

Does he come here often?

Oh no, he hasn't been here for a long time. But he knows the area. He grew up nearby. He indicates with his head. Some of his family are still farm workers. (Sombre eyes, dark eyebrows, full mouth.) But when his mother died in grade nine, he went to stay with an auntie of his in Cape Town.

Oh yes?

He was away for a long time. He's just back from Berlin. He did a residency there. He's a director and a playwright. He's got a play in mind that's set here, in this area. Sort of site specific. He's sitting here for inspiration. (Should she tell him about the woman?) He hopes something will come to him – something from the past, something from the present. Something he can work with. He has an idea, but it's still very vague. And she, does she live here?

She indicates with her head, close by, just below the school. Is he glad to be back? Yes and no. Berlin was out of this world, but South Africa has lots of opportunities. There's a lot to work with here. There are many stories that still have to be told. It's better than it was in his mother's time – no opportunities, all gates barred. As in *zero* opportunities. (He closes his eyes for a moment at the thought of this and shudders, as if someone is walking over his grave.)

They take their leave. Magrieta walks on. One of the lucky ones, she thinks, one of those who made it, who succeeded in overcoming all the obstacles.

*

When one afternoon shortly thereafter she walks past her kitchen window, her eye catches the eye of a man in front of the house, just outside the fence. In the split second that she sees him, she knows the man wants something from her, but he doesn't look like someone she wants to have dealings with. She retreats quickly, moves away from the window, out of his field of vision. But when she cautiously moves forward a while later, he's still standing at the fence. Now she can no longer pretend not to have seen him.

She slides open the window and asks him what he wants. It's someone she hasn't noticed before in the neighbourhood. Lean, sinewy, tough, bare chest, heavily tattooed, fucked-up face, broad over the cheekbones, no front teeth, scar across one cheek. His pants, low over his lean hips, navel exposed, are held up with a rope. When he comes closer, she suddenly looks with sharpened interest – on his chest, yellow-brown like tanned leather, is a tattoo of a rose. Unmistakably a rose, in fine detail, the outlines in blue, the petals shaded a light red; big – it nearly covers his entire left breast, over the cardiac region. He's explaining something. She can't hear. Gardening work? A truck passes, she doesn't hear. Around his neck he wears a fine chain with a small charm. She can't make out exactly what it is. She's alarmed. Perhaps from the woman in the vineyard? She can't remember – did the woman wear a chain, or is she imagining it? No, she says to him through the window, sorry, she has someone who works in the garden. Then she slides the window shut fast and securely and turns away, away from him and any further appeal.

*

A day or two later she walks in the vineyard again along the same road where she met Ashley Fondant. He's there again, but he's not alone, there's someone with him. Also young, but big, solid, much bigger than the delicately built Ashley. He introduces himself as Eddy Plant. An attractive guy. A head full of exuberant black curls, a blushing brown complexion; more Indian than Malay in appearance. So much more blooming than the sombre Ashley.

Is he also in the theatre? No, he's a rapper and visual artist. And what does he do – paint, video, installation art? He's not interested in conventional art forms. He no longer panders to the aesthetics of privilege. He's tired of that, of bending over backwards. Been there. He's now got a different calling. Back to the people. He's an organic intellectual, now. A cultural worker. He does oral poetry and mural art all over the place; he's into people's history. He takes the people's history to them. He's part of a collective. They want to make the people politically woke. They want to bring their history to them in public spaces. They want the people to participate in it. The children and the old ones. The people like it. They work on the Flats and in Khayelitsha.

All this Eddy imparts with an open, engaging smile. He's wearing a soft, faded dark-blue T-shirt, boots, and a kikoi around his sturdy waist. Today the last rays of the sun project a halo around the curly heads of both of them – as of two apostles in a painting.

Ashley isn't listening, he smokes and nibbles at the nail of an index finger. She asks him how his ideas for the play are faring. No, it's coming along, he's seeing something, but he's not seeing it clearly yet. (Sombre gaze cast down.) Something *wants* to come to him, but he's not getting a clear picture yet. So far he's only getting a sense, an atmosphere, he says, closing his eyes, gesticulating vaguely with his hands. Something's coming to him out of the mist. A vision. A revelation.

Twice more Magrieta comes across the two of them when she goes for a walk. Ashley with the fashionable hair and Eddy with the kikoi and faded T-shirt. Each time Magrieta thinks she wants to tell them about the woman – of her apocalypse fatigue and of her cellphone that she threw into the river, and of her mysterious disappearance. But she doesn't. On the third (and last) day Magrieta suddenly has the laughable notion that these two somehow absorbed the woman in the vineyard into themselves – *ingested* is the word that occurs to her. More than that – not a one-sided process, but also as if the woman *allowed* herself to be ingested and in that way *reinvented*. She has to laugh. Such a silly notion.

Eddy looks as if he has absorbed all the rays of the setting sun into his body. His voice is soft for such a large man. He tells her that he's going to be doing a kind of residency in Khayelitsha, starting the next day. He's going to help young artists at the community centre. There's little happening there. He wants to help them to get a few projects going. He'll stay there for a few days in his bakkie.

The afternoon shines beneficently on Magrieta's head and back. The ground hasn't cooled down yet, it retains the day's heat. The vine leaves glow. Everything shines. She should go along some time, she says jokingly to Eddy. They could travel through the countryside in his bakkie. He could bring the people's history to them and she could explain the basic principles of zoology to the children. She can teach them a lot – she knows everything from the worm to the whale!

Eddy laughs and shakes his head. 'It's a possibility,' he says.

Who knows, Magrieta thinks (already a bit dizzied by the shimmer of the afternoon sun), perhaps the ingested woman is sitting high up in one of the trees further along, in a nest of leaves and branches, high as a kite from the shedding of her self. Or otherwise she's long ago wisely decided to call it a day, surrendered the expensive tent and sleeping bag to her fellow pilgrims, cut her losses, and is now sitting in her 4×4 again, the coiffed poodle in the back, reconciled with her alienated husband, daily en route to one of the state-of-the-art morning markets in the area, intent on buying a handmade cheese, a home-baked loaf, a case of bespoke wine and a bunch of freshly picked proteas.

She does not come across them again. Gone are the two cultural workers, to labour on the Flats like (earth)worms and transform them into fertile compost.

Twenty-two

Agent Buitendach lets her know that they are on their way with the whale skeleton. He and Barry Cilliers packed it. Magrieta can just see them in a gigantic truck, the two of them in front in the cab. In the back the precious cargo; all the parts neatly packed into boxes and numbered. So much that could go wrong: the truck could be hijacked, or capsize and catch fire, or hurtle down a steep mountain slope somewhere. But a day later Buitendach reports that they have arrived safely, now the great task awaits: the remounting of all the little parts of the whale. A huge task, but they are excited. As he's mentioned, they never expected such a donation.

Early in November Magrieta tells Markus Potsdam she's going to Albany West to see the installed whale skeleton. She'll also use the opportunity to contact a few associates. Also to liaise with new associates, should that be necessary.

She phones Alta Meyer, the Uber woman, to take her to the airport. On the way they talk about apocalyptic scenarios and the very slight impact of the prostitutes' protest. It didn't even make the papers, the woman says.

Magrieta is eager to see the whale skeleton, but she boards the flight with a feeling of foreboding. She doesn't know what this niggling presentiment has bearing on – on her daughter, on Willem, perhaps on Markus Potsdam? She's read that people emerging from a deep depression commit suicide as soon as they start feeling better because only then do they have enough energy to perform the act.

The feeling is so bad that she almost turns around when she's already on the plane. She WhatsApps Isabel that she must please keep an eye on Potsdam.

Arriving in PE, she rents a car. She arrives in the town in the late afternoon. The university vacation has started, the hostel is once again available for accommodation. As before she stays in the hostel room. Simple as a convent cell.

The town is in the grip of an unusual heat wave. It's as hot now as it was cold during her previous visit.

In the early evening she walks through the quiet, hot town. At a restaurant in the main street she eats a salad, drinks two glasses of wine. She WhatsApps Willem: *Are you okay, I have such terrible premonitions.* He replies: *Of course I'm okay! Forget your premonitions; you've often had them before without anything happening. I'm waiting for you.*

She reads until late in the book she's brought along, *From Bacteria to Bach and Back: The Evolution of Minds*, by Daniel Dennett. The worm definitely also has its place in this great scheme of things. She has a restless night.

Early the next morning she goes to the natural history museum. Agent Buitendach is awaiting her at the door. Behind him is Barry Cilliers with his fuzzy outline. He is an expert in the field of the earliest Stone Age settlements in the Cape, she has since found out.

The skeleton has not been set up in the entrance hall, but in the large hall where the mammals are displayed.

She enters the large space. She expected that the skeleton would be suspended from the ceiling, but it's been skilfully mounted on two high steel stands – one that supports part of the tail, one that supports the skull. In this way the skeleton is lifted so high above the ground that one could almost walk under it. The flipper is *just* above eye level. In a single glance she takes in the gigantic proportions of the fish. It's even bigger than she expected. Something happens in her throat. She slowly takes cognisance of every detail. The massive ribcage, like the hull of a boat. The shoulder blade. The flipper with digits like those of a human hand. The colossal upper and lower jaw, the baleen like two heavy curtains affixed on either side to the upper jaw. The graceful undulation of the caudal and dorsal vertebrae. Bigger, much bigger than she imagined it.

Agent Buitendach and Barry Cilliers stand at a distance, extremely pleased. She says they needn't wait for her. She would like to sit here on her own for a while. Fortunately there's nobody else in the large room.

She counts the ribs. She counts the vertebrae. She paces out the length of the fish. So staggeringly big. Completely off the human scale.

When she's done – for the time being, because she wants to come back – she has tea with the two scientists in the restaurant, as she did the time before. She asks them about the process of packing up, the installation.

That afternoon she goes to have another look at the coelacanth.

The heat is intense. On the way back from the Department of Ichthyology there are Zimbabweans displaying their wares under a shade tree. She orders a skull of glass beads in bright orange from them. She says it's urgent, because she's leaving the day after tomorrow. They promise to have it ready in time.

She won't get to see Nonki Jansen van Rensburg this time – Magrieta has already been told that Nonki has been in hospital for a while and is now convalescing with friends on a farm outside the town. The work in the township took its toll – it seriously impaired her health.

The person she has to contact as a possible new associate is not in town at the moment.

She meets Agent Green in the late afternoon in a coffee shop. She's reached him just in time, he is on his way overseas. There are sunshades outside the coffee shop, but it's so hot that they prefer to sit in the cool, dusky room inside. They first talk about Bureau matters and then she asks him about his writing. Is he still interested in Bizarro fiction and Alt-Lit? Now more than ever, he says. It's given his writing new impetus. (He's clearly not let himself be put off by her dismissive parting words at their last meeting.) While he's enthusiastically explaining with his tantric fingers her attention wanders.

She has a bowl of soup for supper and drinks two glasses of wine again. She sends Markus Potsdam an SMS: *Are you okay, are you keeping your head above water? Don't hesitate to let me know if you feel you can't cope.* Previously she wouldn't have thought of sending him such a personal message, but things between them have altered, and with her premonitions she can't *not* contact him. She knows it's probably ridiculous to send him such a message – if he is planning something, he's not going to let her stop him.

The next morning she goes to have another look at the whale skeleton. Again she is alone in the big room, fortunately. For a long time she just sits on the bench looking at it. She remembers the power with which the living fish propelled itself out of the water. She thinks of the total loveliness of that apparition.

That afternoon she walks with Agent Buitendach and Barry Cilliers to the stone quarry outside the town. She said that she would like to see it close up, she likes stone quarries. It is dead quiet here, and very hot. A large plot of ground is bordered on three sides by the hollowed-out walls of the quarry. Above their heads is the cloudless sky. The colours of the walls are ochre yellow, light and dark grey. The rock walls are steep. On the narrow rock ledges a few little trees are growing. Apart from small bushes there isn't much vegetation.

On the way back they don't talk much.

After she's rested for a while in the afternoon, she goes to see if the Zimbabweans have completed her skull. No, they don't make it themselves, they don't have enough of the orange beads. Somebody has made it in Johannesburg. It's already on its way here by taxi. They assure her it will be in time, she can come and collect it the following morning. She doesn't know how to picture the taxi coming all the way from Johannesburg with her skull of beads. Perhaps it's been posed on the dashboard. Perhaps it's travelling on one of the passengers' lap. Skull as lucky charm.

Willem phones her that evening. He doesn't know if she's heard already, but the guy who visited her the other evening has had a fatal accident. 'What was his name again?'

The news hits her like a blow to the stomach. Her first thought is poor Bertie, the *poor* man.

'Bertie,' she says, 'Bertie Oberholzer. How did he die?'

'Apparently he'd been missing for a few days. His body was found yesterday. Apparently he died on a hike in the mountain.'

'Where did you hear?'

'In the paper this morning. Although he was apparently an experienced mountaineer. The Swiegers fellow he worked with says everybody in the department is very shocked. Nobody expected it.'

'I told you I had a nasty premonition.'

'I wouldn't attach too much value to that, Magrieta, it sounds like a coincidence to me.'

'If you say so,' she says.

'You sound upset,' he says.

'What do you expect,' she exclaims, 'I knew him, he was with us that evening, shortly before!'

'Okay. I didn't realise you had that much contact with him.'

'I didn't. I talked to him a few times. He'd come to me when he was very upset about Swiegers' duck. About other things as well.'

'Now you feel responsible.'

'I don't feel responsible. I'm upset. It doesn't sound like an accident to me.'

'Apparently there's an inquest pending. Bon voyage,' says Willem. 'We'll talk more later. I hope you feel better when you get back.'

'Thank you.' She thinks better of saying it's unlikely.

A strange thought occurs to her. If she had to choose between it being Bertie or Markus, would there be any choice for her? Of course not. She knows she's relieved it's Bertie and not Markus – however sorry she feels for Bertie when she thinks how desperate he must have been. And that maybe – probably – he took his own life just to spite the stupid Swiegers. He should have *known* that Swiegers was so wrapped up in his damn duck that nothing else mattered to him.

The next morning she goes to collect the orange skull from the Zimbabweans, pays for it, gets into her hired car and drives to the airport in PE. There she catches a plane to Cape Town later in the morning.

The skull is much larger than she expected. The proportions are not very attractive – they're actually a bit comical. It looks more like an ape skull than a human. The face is much too long, and the orange far too orange. It makes the skull throb with an inappropriate exuberance.

Twenty-three

Magrieta attends Bertie Oberholzer's memorial service. She's jolted for a moment when she enters the small hall and finds Bertie Oberholzer standing in front in a black suit. It turns out to be his twin brother. This she reads on a small photocopied sheet that's handed out at the door. They must be identical, because when she screws up her eyes it could just as well be Bertie standing there, in a sober black suit, in a parallel universe. The same ruddy complexion and dark eyebrows. Bertie redivivus as pastor of the Jehovah's Witnesses or some other non-Dutch Reformed denomination, it's not altogether clear.

There are not many people. Magrieta takes a seat at the back from where she can watch everybody. A few students, a colleague or two and, in the first two rows, a dispirited little group of people who look like family. One of them, possibly a sister, a short, plumpish woman, cries softly all the time – it looks as if an unquenchable fountain is welling up in her. Deneys Swiegers is there as well. He's sitting diagonally in front of Magrieta. His face is pale, his normally subdued curls are damp and combed back, like that of a bloody 1950s ducktail. And he's wearing a black leather jacket. For God's sake, what's his case? He looks unlike his usual self. Penitent? The transformational effect of remorse? It's not clear. She wonders what the effect of this uncanny resemblance between Bertie and his twin brother is on Deneys. Magrieta hopes he doesn't see her; she doesn't want to make small talk with him today. She's had enough of him and his damn duck. Markus can take over negotiations with him about Bureau matters.

Magrieta is strangely moved. She didn't expect to be. The back of her throat is constricted, suppressed tears making her throat ache. The woman in the vineyard said we are here to help all incarnate beings on their burdensome passage. She doesn't think she did much to ease Bertie's passage. The very least she could have done was to phone him once or twice after his visit to find out how he was doing.

The brother says that Bertie also considered entering the church, like him. But although he eventually opted for a career in science, he always remained a child of God; his faith was unshakeable. Bertie was the best brother anybody could have. He was the clever one. The brother is at times so overcome that he can't talk. He is absolutely convinced, he says, that God was with Bertie in his last, dark hour. (Would the family also have their suspicions, Magrieta wonders.) A pigeon coos outside. A flock of hadedas fly up skirling over the little hall. It's the chickens coming home to roost, in ever greater numbers, she thinks.

Her attention wanders. She thinks of the worm in the damp soil. She thinks of the beautiful abstract patterns of the ventral and dorsal sections. She misses her work in the laboratory. She thinks of her own dead: her troubled father, in his flannels and sports jacket, hat on his head, cigarette in his mouth, worried, next to the car, before they leave on a journey. If she'd been less intransigent towards him in her youth and later, would he have had a less troubled death? Can their mutual incomprehension ever be undone? Does it leave the very slightest impress on the tissue of the universe – the smallest trace, smaller than a molecule, an atom, a quark, slighter than the slightest imaginable smidgeon?

She thinks it could so easily have been Markus Potsdam from whom they were taking their leave today. She shudders when she thinks of the possibility. There is no guarantee that sometime in the future he won't inflict something extreme on himself.

Afterwards tea is served. Magrieta does not want to linger, but an ex-colleague from the Department of Zoology traps her at the tea table.

When she turns to leave, Deneys is standing diagonally in front of her. For a moment they make eye contact over a plate of koeksisters. Deneys is deathly pale, and he looks terror-stricken. Not a trace of his usual balanced, calm gaze. That's what you get, Magrieta thinks, if you're more concerned about mechanical ducks than about the people closest to you.

Before leaving, Magrieta quickly slips into the toilet at the back of the hall. On the door of the toilet is written: YOU CAN STAY AS YOU ARE FOR THE REST OF YOUR LIFE OR YOU CAN CHANGE TO MAINSTAY. Next to it a rough drawing of what could be either a penis or a bottle of Mainstay.

She tells Isabel about this the next day.

'You're lucky,' says the girl, 'that the universe communicates with you like this behind toilet doors. What will you do?'

'What do you think,' says Magrieta, 'I'm going to change to Mainstay, of course!'

'Fuck a buck,' says Isabel.

And that's where they leave it.

*

They turn around. Now Magrieta is lying behind and Willem in front. Her knees in the back of his legs, her stomach against his buttocks. It is late afternoon. The light is fading. There is a cool light in the penumbral room. The wind lifts the curtain slightly. Her left hand slips in under his underpants so that she can get a good firm grip on his buttock. In her right hand she holds the back of his head, which rests in her hand like the half-skull, filled with blood, in one of the four hands of the goddess Kali.

Acknowledgements

My process is organic – while writing I avail myself of a variety of articles in periodicals, on Wikipedia, in books – so divergent that later I can't retrace my own steps. The one source to which I constantly return, however, is Richard Dawkins' *The Ancestor's Tale*. And for *Pikaia* I consulted Stephen Jay Gould's *Wonderful Life: The Burgess Shale and the Nature of History*.

My thanks to my publisher, Nèlleke de Jager, for her continued, un-wavering support and commitment. Michiel Heyns, my true and trusted translator – thank you for making the difficult process of translation such a pleasurable experience. Angela Voges, thanks for editing the manuscript so meticulously. To Andries Gouws, still my most stringent reader.

My thanks, too, to Liesbeth Gouws and Jeremy Levick, who corrected the errors in physics.

And to my daughters, Brink and Liesbeth, who always make me see that it is worth it after all.